# Dangerously Mine

## A.M. Griffin

ELLORA'S CAVE
ROMANTICA®
ELLORASCAVE.COM

An Ellora's Cave Publication

www.ellorascave.com

Dangerously Mine

ISBN 9781419969805
ALL RIGHTS RESERVED.
Dangerously Mine Copyright © 2012 A.M. Griffin
Edited by Briana St. James.
Cover design by Fiona Jayde.
Cover photography by Bomg, Stryjek Amnd, Aleksandr
Doodko/Shutterstock.com.

Electronic book publication December 2012
Trade paperback publication 2013

# Dedication

ﬆ

To my biggest supporters, my mother, my husband Ryan and children; Jori B., Myles and Mia Loren, I love you all. Thank you to Maurice and Arthella for supporting the dream.

# Acknowledgements

ﬆ

Thank you to everyone who made this possible: Dirty Diana for your inspiration and support, Cricket, the MudPuddle, Terri and Stephy, and of course, Bree and EC for giving me a chance.

# Prologue

ℵ

The awful stench coming from her was embarrassing. Eva Smith sniffed under her arms.

*Yep, I can raise the dead.*

The jeans she had on were faded and torn. She had on a t-shirt with a picture of the cartoon characters Orangey and Purple, taken from a scene of one of their Internet webisodes. Even that was no more than tattered rags now. She could only imagine the cartoon characters saying about her stench, *"Gurrl, you stink!"*

The whole reason she volunteered for night watch, again, was to get a break from the stench. The smell from fifteen people who hadn't had a bath in a week was nauseating to say the least.

Eva crouched on a tree branch twenty feet above the forest floor. Years as a martial artist gave her the strength and agility to scale the tree with ease. But now, after hours in the same position, her muscles ached. With one arm hugging the tree for stability, she used the other to punch on the cramp that had formed in her thigh.

She scanned the horizon of clustered trees, looking for camp. Although she couldn't see them, she knew they were there, hiding beneath the canopied covering of the lush trees. Her constant companion, Allysan, sat in the tree opposite hers. Ally didn't dare come closer and even joked that their combined stench would melt the forest surrounding them. Her legs hung underneath her as she hummed *Sun and Moon* by Duk Duk Goose, her favorite Afro-Punk band from New York. The song was appropriate. Because of the enormous spacecraft in the sky, she had not seen either in a while.

Although this wasn't Ally's night to keep watch, she was here to kill the boredom. Eva didn't mind. She welcomed the company of her new friend, especially tonight. The forest seemed weird. *Strange.* She couldn't put her finger on it.

Her senses had been on high alert ever since the aliens came. Her neighbors had been delusional about their arrival. But Eva knew better. While they were busy making "Welcome to Earth" signs, she'd cowered in her barricaded apartment.

Why had they come to Earth? She didn't have a clue, but she had seen enough sci-fi movies to know this would end badly. These extraterrestrials didn't want to "phone home".

They arrived in shiny metallic spacecrafts that sat low in the sky in every major city around the world. As big as small cities, their crafts blocked the sun, forcing residents to live in perpetual darkness.

In less than a week, they'd leveled countries, toppled governments, disrupted communication and swatted the world's most powerful super-nations' military forces down as though they were nothing but pesky flies. All hell broke loose.

Eva had been right, hostile aliens had invaded Earth. Humans weren't prepared for the fight and were losing the battle. Unfortunately, "I told you so" didn't seem appropriate.

That had all happened about three months ago. Or had it been two? No matter, she thought, shaking her head. The small pocket-sized calendar had been lost a long time ago. There was something about running from aliens that made a person decide fast what items were important. The calendar, along with her comb, toothbrush and soap, was long gone.

It was easy enough to pull her jet-black hair back into a bun and scrub her teeth with leaves, but there wasn't an alternative for soap. *Yuck.* Despite soaking in the stream two miles north of camp just yesterday, Eva still felt the fine film of dirt covering her olive-toned skin.

Besides Ally's soft humming, the night was quiet, no signs of nightlife, no owls hooting, no raccoons scavenging, not even a bat in the sky.

That was her first clue that things were about to turn ugly.

"Something's off." Eva scanned the dark horizon. She, along with the others with her, had fled the cities after the initial attack. No one knew why the aliens invaded Earth. Some speculated they were here to enslave humans — or eat them. At this point, it didn't matter.

Survival was the key.

Ally straightened her back and focused her gaze on the skies. "Yeah, I feel it too."

"Go check on everyone. I don't like this feeling." Eva felt the hairs on the back of her neck stand up.

Ally nodded once, scaled down the tree and ran. Eva watched as Ally bounded through the underbrush until her back disappeared in the darkness. Only then did Eva look back to the blackened sky. Something was definitely up.

A familiar low hum filled the still night. *Craft.*

Far on the horizon, a small, metallic craft shot through the sky.

"Shit." She climbed down a few branches. *Too slow.* She scurried faster. Five feet from the ground, she jumped. As her feet hit the dirt and grass, she took off running through the trees to camp, ducking under the low-hanging branches.

As she ran, she could hear her heavy breathing, dried leaves and sticks crunching under her fast-paced feet and the increasingly louder hum of a craft whizzing through the air. It was gaining on her.

"They're coming! They're coming! Take cover!" she yelled. Eva prayed her voice would carry over the loud roar of the craft that now followed close behind.

At the whistle of the craft cutting through the wind above her head, she dove into a thicket of high weeds. She buried her face in the dirt and covered her head and ears with her hands. The noise moved past her.

*Too close.* Her heart slammed in her chest as she jumped up and sprinted to camp. She couldn't leave them. If the craft was taking them, she had to try to help anyone she could.

*Whiz, boom!* The ground shook underneath her feet. *Whiz, boom!* She skidded to a halt. Dirt and grass flew at her, erupting from the ground.

*Whiz, boom!* She shielded her face with her hands. The dirt and rocks pelted her, piercing her skin.

*Bombs.* The impact deafened her ears. Her hands left her eyes and covered her ringing ears. She watched the confusion unfolding in front of her. Blood, skin and body parts were scattered everywhere. Eva looked in horror as most of those who had, in those short months, become dear friends hung dead from tree limbs. A panicked frenzy consumed the bloody and confused survivors.

Hands grabbed her arms tightly, biting into her flesh, shaking her. Her eyes moved to Ally. Tears ran down her cheeks as her mouth moved. *What is she saying?* Eva struggled to understand her.

A bright glow of orange light flickered in the corner of her eye. Her head turned in slow motion toward it.

Her eyes finally focused. *Fire.*

That was enough to snap her out of her stunned daze. "Stick together!" Eva screamed. Panic engulfed those around her. Just as the skittish prey that they were, they spoke all at once, darting in different directions.

"That way!" Eva pointed to the small area free of the rapidly encroaching flames. "Come on!"

Eva made a break for the trees before flames blocked their way. No time to waste. If they stayed where they were, they would surely burn to death. Or worse, get captured. She ran through the small opening with Ally on her heels. She hoped everyone else either heard her command or saw the direction they were heading.

*Whiz, boom!* Ten feet in front of them, the ground shook. Chunks of dirt flew skyward. *Shit!* Eva made a hard left. They needed to avoid the flames quickly overtaking the trees and underbrush.

*Whiz, boom!* Her ears popped, debris pelting her right cheek. Straight, she needed to keep straight. The sounds of her heavy breathing did nothing to block out the screams. *Don't turn around. Lead them to safety!*

Her wild eyes spotting the opening in a clearing in front of her, she skidded and took a hard left. *Avoid the clearing.* They wouldn't stand a chance out in the open.

*Whiz, boom! Shit.* The ground in front of her erupted in a hail of dirt, rocks and grass. The impact knocked her to her back. Without thinking, she scrambled to her feet and ran straight into the clearing.

*Damn.*

The larger craft sat fifty feet in front of them, metallic and shiny with the square door open and a ramp extending from it to the ground. Immediately, she turned around to go back.

"Turn around! Not this way, turn around!" Everyone behind her trampled into the clearing as she tried to push back the way she had come.

No one heeded her warning. "This is all wrong, we need to get out of here," she repeated frantically.

They had been herded.

A monstrous alien with green, scaly skin appeared, towering over her. His yellow eyes with reptilian slits rested on the panicked crowd. He opened his mouth, revealing two-inch-long, razor-sharp teeth, dripping saliva.

"We are the Loconuist."

"No!"

# Chapter One
## *Taken: Year Three*

ᔓ

Heat caressed her face and shoulders. Warmth permeated her body. She could almost imagine the sun's warm rays bathing her in perpetual light and heat. Fresh air circulated through her nostrils. The scent of food wafted through. She sniffed, there was more…

The smell of garbage and feces singed her nose hairs and overrode her senses. Warm liquid with a distinctive metallic taste trickled to the back of her dry, irritated throat. She swallowed. *Blood.*

A dull ache in the back of her head began to throb harder and harder. Voices. *Where are they coming from?* The shouting made her head hurt even more. Straining her ears, she tried to hear what all the fuss was about. Panic rose in her chest, she couldn't understand anything, not a word.

She wasn't on the Loconuist spacecraft.

Feeling more than a little dazed and confused, Eva strained to open her eyes. She snapped one shut when a sliver of sunlight temporarily blinded her. Her heart beat faster. She needed to find out where she was. Sun and fresh air, both were something she hadn't felt in over three years while confined on the Loconuist spacecraft.

She tried again. While one eye wouldn't open at all, the other opened just enough. She winced again. The bright light was too much for her retina. She was right. She was somewhere with sunlight.

But where?

She forced her good eye to open again. A sea of different species were out in front of her, none of them human. A gasp caught in her throat. Aliens! Why were these…things…watching her?

Her eye darted around the crowd. There were some aliens who had the appearance of six-foot-tall walking lizards, others resembled little miniature dragons and, of course, the famous little gray aliens. Sprinkled in the crowd were humanoid figures with hair on top of their heads, two eyes, two arms and two legs. Although humanoid in appearance, the skin colors threw her off. Not the colors she was used to on Earth, but gold, pink, blue and green.

For God's sake, green!

A chill ran down her spine. Eva tried to pull her arms closer to her body, but they wouldn't budge. Looking to her right, a man, or what appeared to be a man, was holding tight to her arm. Another one was on her left. Both men stood just over her five-foot, four-inch frame and were shirtless, their thick muscular frames exposed to the heat. Their brown leather pants were a shade darker than their skin tone.

*This can't be good.*

Finally, her memory returned.

Men, the same as the ones currently holding her, entered the holding bay of the Loconuist spacecraft and dragged everyone out, kicking and screaming. She and Ally were doing what they did best, hiding from the aliens, but that didn't seem to matter this time. These aliens were intent on taking them all away. As they approached Ally and her, the only thing left to do was fight. Fight as though their lives depended on it.

*Guess we lost.*

She'd trained with the best martial artists, and not only was she an expert in various weapons, but also hand-to-hand combat. Her punches and kicks on these guys didn't seem to make a difference. It had been as if she were punching a tree trunk. They were solid as rocks.

"Where's Allysan?" she whispered, her throat hoarse. After all the years trapped in the belly of an alien spacecraft, Ally had become more than her friend. She was the only family Eva had.

Eva tried to open both of her eyes wider, or rather, the one good eye.

The men tightened their hold, twisting her bone in the socket. Excruciating pain surged through her.

"Holy shit! Let me go, you bastards!" She tried her best to wiggle out of their grasp, letting her legs drop from underneath her. No luck. Pain fired up her arms, around and over her shoulders.

Her outbursts did nothing but rile up the crowd. The noise level rose to an almost deafening roar. Pausing a second to comprehend what was really going on, she looked around and stiffened as the realization struck her.

"Are you trying to *sell* me?"

She stood on what she thought was an auction block while the aliens in the crowd appeared to be placing bids on her. Having her arms secured by two thick creatures definitely wasn't helping her situation. She panicked even more, her heart racing. *There's no escape.*

Over the roar, someone shouted her name from her right, the only sound she had understood so far. She spotted familiar faces from the spacecraft behind a large gated area.

"To hell with this," she muttered. Taking two steps back, she swung her arms to the front of her body. The man to her right lost his balance.

*Got you.* She swung both her legs to the right, wrapping her knees around the man's thick neck. Her only chance of escape was to take down the weaker of the two first.

She wasn't sure how much force she needed to snap his neck, but at this moment, she just wanted him down. Her efforts were rewarded as the man slowly slumped to the ground with a thud.

14

The other tugged on her arm, hard. *Snap.* She faltered and yelled out, the pain biting through her.

Definitely dislocated, her left arm would be of no use to her anymore.

Lowering her body, she firmly hit the last man standing, lifting him off his feet. She rammed her useless shoulder just below his belt and sent him flying over her, landing with a hard thud behind her.

Now free, Eva sprinted to the gated area. Her only chance of finding Ally was there. She couldn't get separated from her. Not now. Shutting out the roar from the crowd, she ran as hard as she could.

"Allysan!" Her friend's badly bruised face came into view as she pressed against the gate.

Ally's tears made clean lines down her dirt-stained face. "Don't let them take you away from me!"

"I'm coming!" Eva sprinted hard to the fence.

Ally's lanky arm extended through the links. "Eva! Hurry!"

She reached out to grab the links, and a sharp pain hit her spine. Her legs stopped moving and wobbled under her weight before eventually giving way. Eva could only watch Ally stare back as she fell to the ground. The voice in her head yelled at her to get up, fight against whatever those things had done to her, but her body was no longer under her control.

"No, no, no," Ally cried and begged, dropping to her knees.

"Ally, I'm so sorry."

Then blackness.

# Chapter Two

ဢ

Taio Xochis hated coming to Xenaris. The place was always filled to capacity with traders from all over the galaxy. Everyone knew that if you needed hard-to-find items, go to Xenaris. Right now, he definitely needed a pulson emitter for his disabled vessel.

Their vessel had run into trouble going through the Interplanetary Travel System. Ankon, his pilot, had been lucky to avert a space collision. If anyone could have done it, it was him. In order to return home to Sonis, they needed to get the vessel up to light speed and the only place Ankon could find the part he needed was on Xenaris, the last place Taio ever wanted to be.

Finding what he needed had been easy enough, but it cost as much as a small planet. As soon as the merchants spotted the Sonis Royal Crest on the arm of his black skin suit, they tripled the price.

"How much longer do we have to stay here?" Taio asked. He watched in disgust as a Lorandian thief used his skills to pilfer trinkets off an unsuspecting couple. If the thief had tried that on Sonis, he would have had his hands removed and his lifeless body thrown into the Singha Ocean. With the help of his royal guards, crime was almost nonexistent on the newly developed world.

"Ankon thinks we will be ready to go before nightfall," Rasha replied.

Although Xenaris was a trading planet, it still held many dangers. This place was no Utopia. Taio and Rasha both kept their senses on high alert.

Taio and his crew members all came from Drazlan, the home planet, and had relocated to Sonis, the moon that rotated around Drazlan. Drazlan was hot, humid, sunny and dry and also one of the three sand planets in the Zaronna System. While many thought Drazlan's climate was harsh, they thought Sonis' climate was no better. Because of the harsh climates of the sand planets, the inhabitants all had many of the same characteristics — golden-colored skin, although the tone varied between individuals, dark-colored hair and they were all tall in stature.

"The sooner, the better. This place makes my skin crawl," Taio replied.

Taio, Rasha and some of the other crew members walked through one of the many overcrowded markets on the small dusty planet. The sun was almost unbearable, even for a male who grew up on a planet that circled two suns. He had his shoulder-length hair pulled off his face and secured at the nape of his neck. Still, the sun's rays assaulted him. Xenaris had the harsh climate one would expect from a planet that was set too close to its sun.

The crowd of locals and visitors parted, giving him and his crew a wide berth as they took the time to look for goods that would be needed for the journey home. While the merchants saw unlimited credits when they looked at the royal crest, others saw mercenaries, warriors, guards.

Taio knew the effect he and his crew had on everyone, but there was no point getting back on the vessel just yet. It was docked on a space station, undergoing repairs. So while they waited, some of the crew picked up trinkets for loved ones, while others purchased goods for themselves. Taio purchased a gem necklace for his younger sister, Saia. Of course, the price had been exorbitant, but the necklace matched her eyes.

They walked by a crowd that suddenly went from a small hum to an eruption of roars. "The slave market is in full swing," Rasha noted.

Taio sneered, his lip curled in distaste. He had no desire to stop by the slave markets Xenaris was famous for. In fact, even after forty-one birth cycles, bile rose in his throat at the idea of beings sold as if they were worth no more than an inexpensive trinket or bauble. He could not stand to watch as beings were sold into slavery while others enjoyed the melee it caused.

Slave trading had been outlawed many cycles ago on every planet in this galaxy except for Xenaris. At that time, Xenaris' ambassadors petitioned the Galactic Council to legalize slave trading on their planet. After all, Xenaris was famous for its trading and hard-to-find items. The request had been granted with certain exceptions. Humane protection must be provided for those being sold.

As he was about to pass the podium where the slaves were being held, his eyes caught what had undoubtedly made the crowd erupt. Standing on the platform was a small female fighting two Tresdonians. They were short in stature but made up for it in their dense physical makeup. He'd had the opportunity to take one down during a job when he was still a mercenary. He knew from experience they were not easy to fight.

Yet here he stood, watching the small female use her flexibility to outmaneuver her captors and eventually free herself from their grasp. By the condition of her face, the Tresdonians had a hell of a time getting her to the auction block. She appeared beaten, with a multitude of bruises. He forced in a breath and clenched his fists as he noticed that one of her eyes was most likely lost, the swelling and discoloration of it alone enough to make him cringe. Shame, he thought.

As the crowd roared around him, he stood in awe. Using the muscles in her short legs, she caught one of her captors between them, squeezing her knees around his neck, taking him down. She flipped this way and that, taking full advantage of an arm that was obviously dislocated and useless to unbalance her other captor. With one down, she charged at the other, flipping him over her shoulder. Then she ran.

Taio looked on in puzzlement as the young female ran back toward the slave cage. No one escaped their captors only to run back to captivity. But before she got a chance to reach her destination, the Tresdonian took out a stun gun and shot the fleeing female in her back. She went down with a thud. The crowd went silent.

The Tresdonian advanced. He had to stop this. "Hold your position!"

The Tresdonian had no problem seeing from whom the order had come. Although he stood behind them, Taio towered over everyone in the crowd.

Looking to him, the Tresdonian dismissed his order and continued forward. Taio clenched his fists. He had no problem persuading the slave trader to follow his orders. The crowd parted, making way for him and his crew. Partly in hopes that their entertainment would continue with a new fight, since their prior entertainment was now lying unconscious face down in the dirt.

Taio blocked the Tresdonian's path. "I'm going to assume the thickness of your skull has prevented you from fully understanding my order. I said stand down." Taio spoke the last two words slowly. He placed his hand on the blaster hooked on the side of his belt.

"You have no authority here," the Tresdonian said.

"Actually, as a member of the Galactic Council serving the Galactic Board and as a member of the Royal House of both Drazlan and Sonis, I have the authority to enforce the laws set forth to protect the galaxy." Taio widened his stance, his hand flexing over his *blaster*. Shooting this slave trader would make him extremely happy.

The Tresdonian looked to the sky, as if lost in deep thought. Because of the Tresdonians' thick bone structure, their skulls did not allow for proper brain growth. The

Tresdonian was clearly having a hard time comprehending what Taio had said. His uni-brow scrunched in confusion and a scowl draped across his face. As humorous as the sight would have been on any other occasion, Taio was in no laughing mood.

"Since I don't want you to hurt yourself thinking, I'll give you the breakdown. While slave trading is legal on Xenaris, you broke the law by harming a slave who was not trying to escape."

The Tresdonian widened his eyes. "She was running."

"She was clearly running back to the gate. Not away from it."

The Tresdonian looked down at the unconscious female and then toward the gate. It was apparent he was trying to figure out a way to explain his reasoning for breaking the law. Just because the law was in place didn't mean it was always upheld. Hell, these creatures probably broke the law every day. This Tresdonian just happened to have the misfortune of breaking the law in front of a Galactic Council Member.

As if feeling the stares of the Tresdonian and Taio upon her, the slave in question began to stir slightly. A painful groan crossed her lips. Taio looked down as a delicate, bloodied and filthy hand reached out and wrapped around his ankle. Even in her current state, the female did not give up her fight. The hand gave a weak tug on his ankle, as if she thought she could pull hard enough to make him fall.

She was a small heap of dirt and blood, with black hair fanning out in a matted mess around her. He could not make out any facial features beneath the swelling and grime. The dirty rags she wore were pieced together. But he had to give it to the female — she was a fighter at heart.

"You take her." The Tresdonian smirked, revealing a mouth full of missing teeth.

Head snapping up and coming back to full attention, Taio stared at the Tresdonian, thinking what he heard was a mistake.

"You take her," the Tresdonian repeated.

Nope, he heard right. "I cannot take her. She's your problem." Taio flinched in disbelief at the mere thought of being responsible for a female child.

"You take her," the Tresdonian said again. This time, he slowed down his words as if Taio was the one with a small brain.

"I can't take her with me. I am not here to buy slaves. I am here to make you stop abusing helpless children."

"She yours now. You take her." The Tresdonian walked past Taio back to the holding tank, undoubtedly to bring out another slave to start the auction again.

"I am not here to buy slaves!" Taio yelled at the Tresdonian's back as the crowd began to grow loud.

"You no buy. She free. We punished," the Tresdonian said over his shoulder.

Realizing what had just happened, Taio stared at the retreating Tresdonian in consternation. He was about to move forward to argue his point but was stopped by Rasha's hand on his shoulder.

"It would be useless to argue with him. If you don't take her with you, someone in the crowd will take her or they will come back and get her." Rasha motioned his head in the direction of the Tresdonian. "Either way, she's as good as dead."

"This I know," Taio said, eyes downcast. The female who had just taken on two Tresdonians now lay in a small crumpled heap at his feet.

"What would I do with a child in my care?"

"You could always give her to one of the families on Sonis. Births have been down again this year. There are plenty of couples that would be honored to adopt a child."

Rasha was right, he thought. Maybe this would be a good idea. Although the population on Sonis was growing every year, they still had trouble conceiving and there were very few children being born. More and more people were leaving Drazlan to settle on Sonis, but the small world still lacked enough children.

He devoted a great deal of money to researching the problem, trying to find a solution. Bringing home a young child would make some couple extremely happy.

"You are right, *brosir*," he said, using the native Drazlan word for brother.

Picking up the bundle at his feet, he tried not to cause pain to an already battered body. He met minimal resistance. She expressed her displeasure with slight murmurings as he slung her over his shoulder and carried her away.

# Chapter Three

## ର

*Where are the vibrations coming from?* The constant soft hum faded in and out as Eva struggled to wake. A pulsating sensation stimulated every nerve in her body and seemed to increase as she became more conscious. Her dream about home slowly faded away.

Every fiber in her body felt rejuvenated. She stretched out an arm and hit the side of something hard and metal with a clank. She froze. She laid her hand flat on a solid, cool surface.

*Huh?*

Confusion and fear coursed through her veins as she struggled to open eyelids that felt leaden. *How long have I been out?*

With blurred vision, she looked around her trap. She had reason to panic. She was naked and in some type of white metal box with a glass top. Reaching both arms out to the sides, she could almost fully extend them, but not quite. The top wouldn't allow her to sit fully upright. The glass was a foot and a half from the tip of her nose.

Looking up through the glass, she focused on the stark-white ceiling of the room.

*Where am I?*

The vibrations were coming from the box, making the whole damn thing hum. *Why am I in here?*

Unable to fight her rising panic any longer, she let out a bloodcurdling scream. The sound echoed off the metal walls. It didn't matter if anyone could hear her or not. The panic of the unknown became too much to bear. The mere thought of *why* she could possibly be in a humming box stressed her mind as each second ticked by.

*Calm down.*

She closed her eyes again, trying to control her breathing. She retraced the events that had led up to this predicament. She and Ally had been standing together in the holding bay, waiting to see who would be taken off the craft to God knows where. She remembered that a group of short aliens had come in and started ushering many of the younger women into a separate area of the craft. She and Ally had been among those who had been chosen for the unknown.

Then, the auction block.

*Allysan.*

She could not remember what happened after that, but now there was an urgency to find the woman who had become her best friend, sister and companion.

With renewed energy, Eva opened her eyes. She had to assess her situation if she was going to escape. Placing her hands on the glass in front of her, she pressed lightly to see if it would open.

It wouldn't budge. Locked.

Two golden faces came into view, peering down at her through the glass.

"Ahh!" Startled by their sudden appearance, Eva yanked her hands from the glass.

The two males stared down at her while she stared up at them. It was clear from their skin coloring they were not human, but at least they were humanoid. Their facial features were human enough for her. *Did they come to rescue me?* She dismissed the idea of a rescue just as fast as it had come. Even if they looked human, these males weren't.

*Don't let them fool you, Eva.* She tried to read their intentions as they began to talk to each other in a language she couldn't understand.

She kept her eyes on them. She didn't know where she was or who these men were, but she was prepared to fight if they let her out. She tried to relax her body by concentrating on pacing her breathing. This was the only way to stay flexible and ready. Un-balling her hands, she relaxed them on her chest, instantly feeling the warm, smooth sensation of bare skin.

She snapped her head down. The men above her were taking in the full, unrestricted view of her naked body. She had forgotten all about her lack of clothes. *What the hell is going on here!* She maneuvered one arm over her breasts and the other hand to cover her pubic area.

"No freebie peep show here!" she yelled. "Nothing to see, move along." She wished it would be that easy to send them on their way.

It was obvious she had not been successful at escaping the auction block. These men had bought her and were now holding her captive to use as a sex slave.

"Ha! You wasted your money, buddies. I'm nobody's sex slave. I'd rather die and take one of you with me than give in to this."

Her voice vibrated off the wall as she continued to bellow her thoughts about the situation to the men on the other side of her confinement.

"I see that her voice has returned." Rasha peered down at the female in the healing tank. "What do you think she is yelling?"

"I can't understand her dialect any more than you can," Taio said, trying to keep his voice even. He feared it would crack as though he were a youngling seeing a naked female for the very first time.

His body still reacted the same way it did the first time he had seen her cleaned and placed in the healing tank. His heart quickened, his stomach flipped and his cock hardened at the mere sight of her. He had been relieved when Ship informed him that the child he had been ogling was really an adult female.

That had been two rotations ago—since then, he'd checked on her progress every day. Sometimes multiple times a day. Her species did not look much different than his. She was smaller, with long, silky black hair and skin toned lighter than his. But the best news of all was that she matched him anatomically.

He watched her perky breasts rise and fall with the rhythm of her breathing. He couldn't wait to cover her large brown nipples with his mouth. The dark hairs nestled between her legs seemed to beckon for his fingers.

"I know you can't. I was wondering what she could be saying. Do you think she is trying to thank us for saving her?" Rasha asked.

Taio hid his smile. She was trying to shield herself from him. It didn't matter. The memory of her delectable body was burned forever in his mind.

He could imagine his hands holding onto her hips, helping her rise up and down on his cock. His gaze traveled down to her shapely legs. He imagined running his tongue along the length of them.

Suddenly aware that Rasha was looking down at his female and seeing her naked just as he was, he straightened, taking his eyes off the healing tank and looking at his second-in-command. He didn't know if Rasha had similar thoughts, but he needed to claim her as soon as possible. When Rasha didn't immediately straighten and look up, Taio peered at him through the slits of his eyes.

Finally straightening, Rasha looked at Taio with a confused look on his face.

"I find it strange that we do not know her dialect. Ship cannot find a trace of it in the databanks."

Knowing his longtime friend was truly puzzled and did not have thoughts that ran to the lascivious, Taio relaxed a little.

"Ship is contacting other vessels in the area of Xenaris to find out where she came from. Once that is done, we will be able to get a dialect on her."

Just then, Ship's voice spoke throughout the cabin.

"I have received multiple reports regarding the female's species. The reports state the Loconuist originally brought her race to this sector. I am currently trying to locate the Loconuist vessel to obtain additional information."

"Thank you, Ship," Taio said.

If anyone could find out about the female's unknown race, it was Ship. The entity would find him the information he needed.

But it didn't solve the problem at hand. He had to let her out of the healing tank whether he understood her or not. That was what prompted Rasha and him to the infirmary in the first place. Ship had alerted them she was waking up. He had wanted to be on hand to explain where she was and what had happened to her firsthand.

"Well, should we let her out?" Rasha asked, looking down at her through the glass.

Taio pressed the button that would open the glass door as wild eyes stared back at him.

# Chapter Four

## ဆ

It took all of her training to pace her breathing as she watched the glass top silently slide down a hidden track. She lay in place, staring as the top slowly opened, freeing her from the metal coffin. Determined as she was to focus on keeping her breathing under control, she couldn't ignore the two overly large males staring down at her.

She willed her eyes from the sliding glass top to focus on the males. Both of them were huge and extremely muscular. Well, muscular may have not been the right choice of words. These men would have put Arnold Schwarzenegger to shame.

They each had an elaborately designed tattoo that covered one side of their faces. The tip of a light-blue and indigo-colored wing covered the cheek of one of the males and extended down his neck and chest, his shirt obstructing her view of the rest of the picture. Rising from underneath the other man's shirt up his neck was a dark-blue animal arm with red scales on it, its claw wrapped around his right eye.

Although similar, each man had distinguishing characteristics. One looked at her with curiosity, the other with fire in his eyes. One was handsome, but the other was downright gorgeous. Not model gorgeous. His features were too sharp and hard for modeling. His lips were full, with high cheekbones that rose to lavender-colored eyes surrounded by dark, full lashes a girl would die for.

Interrupting her thoughts, the male with the tip of a wing tattooed on his face said something to her that she didn't understand. When she looked at him without replying, he repeated the words again.

"I don't understand you." She shook her head. The males turned to look at each other. The same male leaned in closer to her and repeated himself again. This time a lot slower than the first.

"Are you serious?" she added, irritated.

"I don't think she can understand me," Rasha said.

"And if you ask her again, she still won't be able to understand you."

"At least I am attempting to communicate with her. All you do is stand gawking."

Taio rounded on Rasha. "I do not gawk! Ship said it couldn't determine her dialect. It would be pointless to try to engage her in some type of conversation. I'm not the one who insists on asking her the same question over and over, even after it is apparent that she does not understand."

Without warning, the female grabbed the side of the healing tank and propelled herself out, planting a foot firmly in his stomach before landing on the floor.

Caught off guard, Taio let out a grunt and doubled over as the wind was forced from his lungs. After landing, she quickly scanned the room.

Rasha reached out and tried to grab her arm. Maneuvering away from him, the female sidestepped out of his reach and ran to the other side of the healing tank.

Assured with the distance that she had put between herself and them, she again scanned the room.

"Calm down. We are not going to harm you." Rasha raised his arms in the air.

"Great Ancients! What are you doing?"

He had known Rasha all of his life. Rasha's father had been one of his father's diplomats and Rasha had been a constant figure in their palace. Never had he seen Rasha throw up his hands in surrender.

"Can't you see that I am trying to get her to calm down? She fears us."

"We are not the ones who jumped out of the healing tank and attacked her."

Rasha waved his hand in the air dismissively. "Having this female kick at you would hardly be considered an attack."

Rasha turned to the female. "We will not hurt you." He raised his hands again, ignoring Taio.

She was short, but he hadn't expected a grown female to be as short as she was, standing just below his armpit. Every time she turned side to side in a frantic motion, her firm breasts swayed and jiggled with movement.

*Great Ancients.*

If she didn't stop moving, his pants would burst open. She turned in a tight little circle, taking in the full view of the room. Taio got a good view of her backside for the very first time. Her butt, just like her breasts, was high, round and voluptuous. A small groan escaped his lips.

When she turned back to face them, her breasts swayed from the abrupt stop and continued to sway for a little longer.

"Awww…" he murmured. He was going to spill his seed right here in the healing bay.

Her hands flew back up to cover herself. Rasha looked over at Taio. Then down at the bulge that was straining against Taio's pants.

"You are not going to tell me you are in the least bit interested in that small female." Rasha's eyebrows rose.

"And of course you are going to stand there and tell me that the naked female before us is not at all appealing to you?"

"She is the size of a child!" Rasha said, his voice rising. "You had plans to give her to one of the families who work in the kitchens as a gift for their loyal service."

"It's now clear, as evidenced by those gorgeous breasts swaying in front of us, that she is not a child." Taio waved a hand at Eva. "And if she keeps swaying about that way, I am going to burst through my pants," Taio mumbled. He couldn't help it if his cock had a mind of its own.

"Try not to jump on her while I find her some clothes." Rasha walked to the closet.

Eva and Taio were left facing each other. He thought if he willed hard enough, maybe one of her breasts would pop out from under the arm that currently blocked his view.

She pressed her arm harder across her chest and lifted her head defiantly under his heavy gaze.

Taio crossed his arms over his chest. They seemed to be at a standstill before Rasha came back to his side.

"We don't have anything that will fit her. All I could find was a meditation shirt. It should still be long enough to cover her up." Rasha held up the shirt, inspecting it.

"This is for you to put on." Rasha held it over his head and pretended he was putting it on. After he was finished with his instruction, he tossed it on the healing tank, closer to her side so she could easily grab it.

She reached down and grabbed the shirt and swiftly put it over her head.

"Ra-sh-a." He elongated his name and pointed to his chest.

"Ra-sh-a," she replied, mimicking his pronunciation.

The shirt enveloped her, hanging down to her calves. The sleeves were so long she had to roll them up so she could have some use of her hands.

"Ta-io." Rasha pointed to Taio's chest.

"Ta-io." She mimicked his pronunciation.

"Ee-va." She pointed to herself.

"Ee-va," Rasha repeated.

They both turned toward Taio, waiting for him to say her name, but he just stood watching her with his arms across his chest. He didn't need to know her name for what he had planned for her. When he gave no indication of trying to say her name, she rolled her eyes and looked away. He smiled. She was feisty. He was finding that he liked his females feisty.

"I have news on the visitor called Ee-va," Ship announced over the vessel's intercom system.

Clearly startled, she struck a defensive stance and looked around the room for the source of the voice. Immediately seeing her distress, Rasha began to make soothing sounds, trying to calm her down. Taio was officially disgusted with his friend and fellow warrior's sudden decline.

"What information do you have on her?" Taio asked.

"Ee-va is from a planet called Earth. It is in a very distant galaxy from ours," replied Ship.

"How did she get to this galaxy?" Taio asked.

"The Loconuist colonized Earth and started to transport the Earthlings off their home planet to other galaxies. They are in the process of stripping the planet. Since the colonization, the Loconuist have made a substantial amount of wealth with the sale of the planet's natural resources and inhabitants. Earth is the only inhabitable planet in its solar system. Since this is the case, there are billions of inhabitants on the planet alone," Ship said.

The Loconuist were relentless in their pursuit to find worlds that were not as advanced. They often went to other worlds under the false pretense of trade. Once they gained the trust of the people, they then infiltrated and took over the world's governing body, taking control and wiping out the entire planet and inhabitants. Sometimes they left the inhabitants on the planet to slave for them or whatever was needed.

Since slaves were in high demand these past cycles, he could see why they had begun to sell Earth's inhabitants. The Loconuist could sell the weaker inhabitants and still keep plenty on the planet to mine and farm as needed.

"What else could you find out about her?" Taio asked.

"I cannot tell you anything more specific about her. I am still trying to find a dialect that is a match, or at least a close match to hers. If you could get her to talk more, it would help me to complete that task."

"What about her age?" Taio asked.

"Her age according to a bone scan is marked as thirty-four Earth cycles. Earth rotations and cycles are faster than ours. She is twenty-two birth cycles on our own world."

Just as Ship was finishing the last sentence, Jor'Dan entered the room. Eva didn't waste any time before bolting toward Jor'Dan and the open door.

Taio reached out for her. "Don't let her pass!"

# Chapter Five

ഏ

A millisecond was all she allowed to look at her pursuer before turning back to focus on the exit.

She could only assume the giant was telling his friend to stop her. Her mind concentrated only on an escape. She had no clue where she was going. Hell, she didn't even know where she *was*. The details could all be worked out later.

She launched herself feet first toward the man standing in the doorway. Her right hip hit the ground and she slid, breezing between his legs.

Cleared and outside the room, Eva sprang to her feet and took off down the corridor as fast as she could, her bare feet hitting the cold floor, each step smacking hard as she ran. She needed to get away; the thought repeated on a loop in her head. She ran frantically as the heavy footsteps of her pursuers followed behind her.

Down the corridor she ran, her right hand extended out to the wall, searching for an automatic door. On the Loconuist spacecraft, the doors opened by some kind of sensor-detecting movement. She prayed these doors might operate on the same principle.

A door opened as she passed it. She wasn't surprised but prayed a silent thank you. Taking one good look behind her and not seeing her pursuers in sight, she ducked inside the dark room.

The darkened room immediately brightened, her entrance causing the automatic lights to activate. With a swoosh, the door slid closed behind her. Turning in a full circle, she eyed her surroundings. The medium-sized room held crates of various sizes. Good enough place as any to hide.

She took off to a far corner. Satisfied that the room would serve her purpose for now, she dropped to a sitting position, grabbed her knees to her chest and wrapped her arms around them tightly.

As sweat dripped from her brow and her body shook, she waited for two things to happen. The first, for the motion-sensor lights to go off. The second, for the giants to come through the door and get her. *Crap.*

Finally, the footsteps and shouts of her pursuers came from the corridor beyond the door and they were getting closer. Her forehead pressed painfully to her knees, breath ragged, she waited.

The sensor lights blinked off, leaving the room pitch black.

She held her breath. The footsteps were now just beyond the door. Her captors were close enough for her to hear them talking in harsh, deep voices. Not knowing what was said only added to her anxiety.

She imagined every sentence they spoke as "Catch the woman so we can all take turns raping her". *I'll kill them first.* Against her will, her body began to tremble harder. She waited for the inevitable.

Her recapture.

The blood pumped loudly through her head, rushing through her brain and ears, the wait was almost unbearable.

*Be calm.*

She needed to be in control, no matter what happened next. She concentrated on her breathing, imagining the slow, deep breaths of air circulating through her lungs first and then to her body. Within minutes she calmed. Her eyes slowly opened. Staying perfectly still, she strained her ears, trying to locate any other noise beside her own.

Silence. She let out a deep breath.

Eva sat as still as she could. Although calmer, her breathing had not returned to normal. Her chest burned with pain. Her eyes were fixed on the door. She had escaped. But where was she?

"Ally, where are you?" she whispered. "I can't get to you if I don't know where you are. Hell, when you tell me where you are, tell me where I am, so I can go to where you are and then we can both go somewhere away from here."

"That phrase does not make sense," a disembodied voice interjected.

Eva jumped up, her movement causing the lights to click back on. Her eyes darted around the room. She was alone. "Who are you?" She spun, looking for the source. It was the same voice from earlier.

"My name is Ship. Why is your head jerking? Shall I call for help?"

"No!" she yelled. "No," she said again, catching herself and dropping her voice back down to a whisper. "Wait. How is it possible that I can understand you?"

"We placed a Universal Translator in your brain." Eva's hands immediately flew to her head. "Don't worry. You were not harmed. It is standard procedure for all intelligent life forms who travel off-world to be equipped with a Universal Translator."

"So I can understand what those men are saying to me now."

"Because we were unfamiliar with your dialect, there may be some variations in translation, but it should translate effectively for the time being. You will be able to read other languages as well. I can adjust it remotely as I come to understand your language better."

"You will not go into my head!" she said, her voice low and harsh, now more alarmed than ever.

"I told you before, no harm will come to you."

Her eyes wandered around the room, still trying to figure out where the voice came from. "Who are you?" she asked again.

"I told you, my name is Ship."

"I'm on a ship?"

"You are on a vessel. More precisely, you are on the *Saia II*. But to answer your previous question, my name is Ship."

"Oh." She paused for a minute to gather her thoughts. "Where is the ship taking me?"

"You are riding in the *Saia II*. It is more accurately referred to as a vessel."

"I don't get it. You said I was on a ship called the *Saia II*."

"No. The vessel is called the *Saia II*. My name is Ship. I am the entity that sometimes inhabits this vessel."

"And you said I didn't make sense. Sheesh."

"Do you need further explanation?"

"No, well, yes. Just explain the entity part."

"I originate from beings that require an electric current to survive. We operate and control whatever the electric current is running through. We would not be visible to your eyes. We have been around since well before your time," Ship explained.

"So right now you are in this ship, err, vessel and control it?"

"That is correct."

"So what's your name?"

"Ship."

# Chapter Six

ଊ

"Wait a minute. The ship is the object you live in, not your name. I'm asking you your name. Not what objects you inhabit," she said.

"My name is Ship. Cycles ago, I inhabited a small electrical toy vessel that Taio had as an infant. He named me Ship. I liked it and have used that name ever since."

"Cycles?"

"Yes, you would recognize the meaning as year."

"How long have I been here?"

"Two Sonis rotations."

"Huh?"

"Days."

"Oh. So, what was your name before Ship?" She relaxed back against the wall.

"My name was…"

A high-pitched squeak resonated throughout the room. Covering her ears with her hands did little to block out the shrieking noise.

"I am sorry if my name caused you pain. I will have to add that your ears are sensitive to high-pitched sounds to your information."

"Don't. Ever. Do. That. Again." As her hearing slowly came back, she opened and closed her mouth and rocked her head from side to side.

"I made a note of it. It will not happen again."

"Taio, he was one of the men chasing me. Who is he?" Eva held up her hand. "And if you can't answer without making that God-awful noise, then please don't answer."

"Taio is himself. He does not have an entity inside him."

"Right," she said sarcastically. "I was asking who he was, as in…never mind."

Ship fell silent for a minute.

"I misunderstood your question. Taio Xochis is the first King of Sonis, first son of King Xochis of Drazlan and Prince of Drazlan. He is the owner of Sonis Mercenary and Sonis Gold."

Okay, so she had been sold to some type of royalty. Royalty whom she had assaulted, can't forget about that.

"Are you his sl… I mean, is he your mas…" She blew out a breath. "Do you belong to him?"

She had trouble trying to find the right words to ask. Somehow asking, "Are you a slave?" or "Are you owned by someone?" didn't seem quite polite.

"No. I am my own. We are…friends is the word I believe your people would use."

"So, did he buy me on that planet?"

"From what I was told, you were given to him by the Tresdonians."

"I was given to him. As in free?" *What the hell?*

She couldn't believe it. It's not that she wanted to be sold into slavery, but to be given away. Well, that brought back some bad memories. Damn Tresdonians.

"You proved to be more trouble than you were worth." Ship laughed, a deep rumble that filled the room. Apparently he amused himself.

"That's not very funny. No one had the right to give me away," she said, her voice a low whisper.

Her parents had given her up for adoption when she was two years old. Who gives up a two-year-old? Of course, she didn't want to be sold and bought by anyone, but at least it proved she was worth something. Free, well, that was just...nothing.

A soft clinking sound in the distance brought her out of her downward emotional spiral. She grew quiet and strained her ears. The noises trailed off down the hallway before finally dying down completely. Only then did she turn her attention back to the entity. He wasn't an immediate threat.

She decided to take her chances and keep asking questions. This was more information than she'd gotten from anyone about anything in the past three years.

"Can you please tell me where I am? You told me I'm on some type of vessel, but I really want to know where I am." More importantly, how far away was she from Earth?

"You are in the Delta System."

"Umm...and that is where exactly?"

"The Delta System is ten light cycles away from the Zaronna System. Both are located in the Torus Galaxy."

"Hmm...I need you to be a bit more specific. I need information I can use."

"That was information you could use," Ship said, sounding a bit offended. "We are on our way to the Zaronna System."

"Why are we going there?"

"We are returning home. Your new home. The moon Sonis."

She inhaled sharply as the information settled. *Her new home.* That's what the entity had said.

She shook her head violently. "No. That's not right. My home is on Earth. Can you turn the sh...vessel around and take me back to Earth? Please." The plea tumbled out of her mouth before she could stop it.

"Earth. It is the third planet from a sun located in what your species have named the Milky Way Galaxy. Earth was colonized by the Loconuist just over three Earth years ago.

Since that time, three-fourths of Earth's population has been sold into slavery throughout the Holantis Galaxy, Oli Galaxy, Zinarcarin Galaxy, Istenoru Galaxy, Qeiktig—"

"Stop!" she yelled. Not being able to take any more, she dropped her head into her hands. "Where did you get this information?" she asked in disbelief. He had to be wrong.

Those bastards sold three-fourths of Earth's population? No, that couldn't be true. He was making this up. This had to be a mistake. *All those people...*

"When you were brought onboard, Taio had me check your origins. The Loconuist vessel gave me the information available on your kind."

All of a sudden, the events from the past three years came crashing down on her. The alien invasion, her capture and being separated from people she had come to call friends.

Separated.

Alone.

Again.

Those three thoughts crushed down on her as heavy as a weight.

"I am sorry for your loss." The sincerity in the entity's voice made her believe he somehow understood all she had been through.

She buried her face in her hands and cried. For the first time, she cried for the loss of her planet, her world, her fellow humans and her best friend. The tears poured down her face and spilled on the floor. Her body shook and rocked with grief, the years of turmoil finally being released.

She wasn't sure how long she cried, thankful the entity allowed her to wallow in her pain. Pulling herself together, she wiped her face on the large shirt and squared her shoulders.

"Did he purchase any others?" She was almost too afraid to ask, but afraid not to.

"No, you are the only one. He did purchase two other items from local merchants. Do you wish to know what they were?"

"No. Thank you," she said halfheartedly. "Will I be the only human on Sonis?"

Ship paused. "I don't understand. All the reports I received stated you were from Earth, not from human."

"No. Yes. No. I mean, I am from Earth, but we are called humans. As in the human race."

"I was not aware that other beings lived on Earth besides Earthlings. Well, not until before the Loconuist colonized Earth."

"No, there wasn't. I mean, are there any other Earthlings besides myself on the planet?"

Eva was beginning to understand she had to be more specific with her questions, because she was getting the urge to rip a control panel out of the wall just so she could have the sensation of strangling the entity with her bare hands.

"Sonis is not a planet. It is a moon. And no, you are the only one."

A lump formed in her chest. She would live on a moon with aliens. Would they look the same as the men who chased her or the aliens in the crowd on that planet of hell? She shuddered at the thought.

She pushed the thought from her head. If Ship could find information on her, he could find Ally, right?

"How would I find a friend who was on that planet with me? Is there a way to find out who she was sold to?"

"That would be almost impossible. Slave trading is legal on Xenaris. The transaction does not require the name of the person being sold. All transactions are final. There is no return policy. Are you contemplating returning?"

"No. I wanted to know how to find my friend." Her heart dropped to her stomach.

"Good. You are much safer here than you were on Xenaris. You required extensive repair. You required immediate help, even before I was able to find out anything regarding your genetic makeup. You were broken in many places. I hope I programmed the healing tank to put you back correctly."

Eva jumped quickly to her feet and inspected herself. As Ship talked, an image of Frankenstein's monster came to her mind. In her head was the voice of a mad scientist yelling, "It's alive! It's alive!"

"What is the name of the person you are looking for?" Ship asked, oblivious that Eva had her shirt over her head, making sure all her lady parts were in order.

"Allysan Miller. Hey! Where is my bellybutton?" She dug her finger in her stomach where her bellybutton had once been.

"What is a bellybutton?"

"It's the indention of a hole that I had in the middle of my stomach. It's from my umbilical cord." She scratched at the skin in hopes it was still there, hidden underneath.

"Interesting that you would want a defect back," Ship pondered.

She inspected her legs and knees, the childhood scars now erased. She wiggled her toes, all accounted for.

*Oh my God! What if he closed up the "holes", thinking they were defects?* Eva slid her hand between her legs, trying to inconspicuously check herself. Two holes, all in order. She blew out a breath.

"Taio is becoming very upset that I won't tell him where you are hiding," Ship finally said.

She put her shirt back down and looked up. "Is he still looking for me?"

"Yes. Taio, Rasha, Jor'Dan and Ankon were pursuing you when you fled the healing bay. Why did you run?"

"I had to get away. They were fighting over who was going to rape me first."

"I assure you that was not the case."

"Oh." Honestly, she had forgotten about them for just a moment at least. "Has he been looking for me this entire time?"

"Yes."

"Why haven't you said anything to them? I mean, about where I am?"

"I thought you needed some time to calm down before you encountered them again. I told him you were frightened. I would guess they are all considerably larger than any of the males that would be found on your home planet," he explained.

"Yes, well, they were kinda big. Giant, actually." So far, the three males she came into contact with on the vessel had to be seven and a half feet tall or taller.

"Do you want him to come here to collect you?" Ship asked. Before she could reply, he added, "No, you most definitely would want to go to him."

Eva thought about it for a few seconds before replying that she wanted to go to him. The thought of being hunted down made her want to throw up. At least she could go to him with her head held high and ready to face her future head on.

But angry was a mild understatement. When she finally reached the room where Taio and a handful of his men were, he looked beyond angry.

"He will not harm you," Ship said to her softly. As she walked closer, Taio's lavender eyes glared at her, a scowl on his face and arms crossed over his muscled chest.

"Tell that to him." She nodded in his direction.

# Chapter Seven

## ജ

Taio kept his eyes on Eva as she ate. The dining hall was capable of holding thirty guards and was currently empty except for him, Eva and five others. Although nearly empty, he noticed she positioned herself as far away from him as she possibly could, as if she thought the distance would save her from him. Humph, not hardly. The only reason he let her keep her distance was because of Ship. Otherwise, he would have flung her across his shoulder and taken her to his bed three rotations ago, after her release from the healing tank.

Even though she sat at the table by herself, he could hear her talking. Eva had since exchanged the oversized shirt for a smaller skin suit.

The suit was his sister Saia's from when she had traveled with him a few cycles back. It was obvious Eva had trimmed the bottom to accommodate her short stature. But otherwise the suit was tight in all the right places. Her breasts strained against the material as if they would explode out at any moment. The thought made his cock twitch with anticipation.

She wore her dark hair pulled back in a tight bun on the back of her head. He opened and closed his fingers, imagining them undoing the bun and running his fingers through each silky strand. He was sure it was just as soft as it looked.

Since she sat by herself, he could only guess she was in deep conversation with Ship. About what, he had no idea. He caught snippets of her words every now and then. Some words he understood, others he did not. Ship was in the process of updating the Universal Translator to accommodate the new language. Ship requested that Eva talk as much as possible so he could work out the nuances of the funny language from her home world.

As if sensing his stares, she glanced quickly in his direction. The words on her luscious lips trailed off mid-sentence. He should have turned his head, but didn't. No need to, she would be his soon. He had claimed her. His crew had already been warned to stay away from the human female.

Blue eyes, the same color as Sonis' Singha Ocean, blinked once, then twice, before turning away. Her small head shook, gesturing no, undoubtedly to Ship. He was sure he would hear about it later. Ship would not be pleased with him. He'd promised Ship he would stay away from her while she became acclimated to the new culture she would be thrust into.

"What are your plans for her when we reach Sonis?" Jor'Dan asked.

The younger guard sat down on the bench next to him and chewed on a piece of dried meat. Jor'Dan stood half a head shorter than him and his build wasn't as thick as Taio and Rasha's. Instead of pulling his long hair to the nape of his neck as most of the guards preferred, Jor'Dan displayed his freely. He still had a lot to learn. Even though the females seemed to prefer his hair wild, it was not advantageous for fighting.

"She will be mine."

Jor'Dan nodded in response. "Since you have threatened death to anyone who approaches her, I already suspected that."

Jor'Dan had been with him for over ten cycles, working his way from hired mercenary to royal guard. Next to Ship and Rasha, Jor'Dan could be counted as one of his most loyal friends.

"I will keep her with me for the time being. She has no family to protect her."

"And you are keeping her only because she needs protection?"

"You were a witness to what happened to her on Xenaris. She was almost killed. She needs a protector."

"By the way you are staring at her, I would gamble you have more than protection on your mind."

"Once Ship has all the information he needs, I will claim her in every way."

Jor'Dan looked over at Eva; Taio sensed his friend was trying to see her through his mentor's eyes. "But she is so...small. If the rest of her race is as small as her, it would explain why they fell against the Loconuist."

"Although small, she fought as a warrior."

"What of finding a mate? Is that on hold for the time being?"

Taio shook his head. "I will continue my search for a mate. The people of Sonis are counting on me to provide a strong bonding contract. Until then, the human will make a nice concubine."

Sonis had been given to him by his father for his twentieth birth cycle. At that time, Sonis had been inhabited by only a small group of settlers, those who could stand intense heat and constant dryness.

His father, the King of Drazlan, had been very pleased to get rid of the upkeep and responsibility of caring for it. But unbeknownst to the king, underneath the intense heat and dry sand lay one of the largest gold deposits in the galaxy. Now Sonis was its own very wealthy world.

"And you are sure she will be agreeable to such an arrangement?"

"Her agreement is not required. I own her."

"Since when do we own slaves?"

Jor'Dan was right. His people had never had a history of slave trading, but the thought of giving up his new find clouded his judgment.

"I think you need to bed her. Get it over with and let her go," Jor'Dan said.

Taio watched her intently from across the room. "I plan to." But he did not have plans to let her go any time soon.

* * * * *

Eva pressed her face against the rectangular window in the training room, watching the lights of unknown origin whiz by. She was in one of the training rooms that Ship had sequestered for her. After lunch, she was feeling more than a little stir-crazy. She needed to work off some of the tension that coiled around her muscles. It took all her strength not to get up and leave the dining hall while Taio's gaze bored through her back. Did he really have to keep sending those smoldering looks her way?

His lavender eyes locked on her whenever she entered a room. It was unnerving to be able to feel the heat from them surge through her, making her body feel on fire. The intensity of his gaze made her body respond in a way that she didn't want it to. Every now and again, she wasn't able to resist their pull and would return his stares, only to catch herself before quickly turning away.

No one would ever consider her to be a coward. But there was something about the way he looked at her that had her frightened. And that tattoo on his face. Sometimes it intrigued her and other times it made her scared. Who would allow such an intricate drawing to be completed? The pain alone would have been enough to deter any sane person from getting it, alien or not.

His body was a whole different story. It was downright criminal to have a body like his. The man had a body that would make a nun want to sin. He was tall, unbelievably so, but he was all rippling muscle.

This vessel was full of men and the only one who would give her a second glance was Taio. The thought should have given her some type of comfort. Instead of beating off twenty men, there was only one she would have to worry about. There was no mistaking his intentions. Every time he looked her way, it was as if he were willing her clothes to fall from her body. Her only counterattack so far was to stay away from him.

But she did have to agree with Ship, being under the care of Taio was for the best right now.

Learning about their culture had been a shock. Ship was very forthcoming with his information on Sonis, and especially how the males and females had traditional duties straight out of the eighteen hundreds. She was fed, the dining hall was open around the clock, which was a plus. Oftentimes she found herself standing in front of the computer, requesting the *buro* flank with *nitlick* soup after everyone else was fast asleep. These were the closest thing to Earth food she could find. They had the same taste as chicken and tomato soup.

She was finally clean. Although she would have loved to feel the caress of running water on her skin again, the ionized shower hit the spot. She had clothes, which, although they were tight, were at least clean. And most of all, she didn't feel her safety was in any type of jeopardy, not at the moment. She wanted to find Ally, but she had to face the hard facts.

She was far away from home.

In an alien world.

No money whatsoever.

Nowhere to go.

And alone.

Ship promised to keep his channels open and alert her if he came across any leads on Ally. That gave Eva some type of hope. Ship explained that he would be able to find Ally a lot faster than she ever would. And for some reason, she trusted him. She hadn't felt this way with anyone else she'd encountered so far.

Including Taio.

Finally, pulling herself away from the window, she pulled a training bag from the corner to start her workout. Hand-to-hand combat always made her feel primal, the main reason she loved it so much.

Within minutes, her training suit clung to her body, the lightweight material not constricting her movements at all. Perspiration covered her from head to toe, her once- tied-back hair hanging wet and loose around her. Her muscles thrived under the workout, coming alive once again.

Heavy breathing behind her caught her off guard. She flipped away, landing in a fighting stance facing the intruder.

Taio stood in the doorway, watching. He gave a curt nod her way, the acknowledgement doing nothing to make her feel relaxed.

"You have good skills, Eva." He hooked his thumbs in the waist of his pants and leaned on the doorway. Her name never sounded better.

"Thank you." She relaxed and straightened, her eyes still watching him. This was his first time speaking to her since their ill-fated first encounter.

She didn't dare move closer, especially since she still didn't know his intentions. She didn't move away either, fearing he would view that as a sign of weakness. So she stood her ground, her body betraying her in the worst way. Her heart sped up a little and her breathing became more labored. Now she found her nipples hardening as her name rolled off his tongue.

*I know trouble when I see it.*

Eva willed her body to fight against whatever "mojo" he was throwing at her.

Taio walked into the room and took a sword off a rack on the wall. He began flexing it, testing its weight. The gesture caused his arm and chest muscles to ripple with each movement. *Jesus.*

"Who taught you fighting moves?"

"My sensei, he lived back home." Not a day went by that she didn't think about the elderly Japanese man who referred to her as *kodomo*, or "little child".

"Earth," he said as a statement, rather than a question.

"Yes, Earth. Ann Arbor, Michigan, more specifically."

She eyed the weapons on the wall. She was trained to use various fighting weapons — sais, kamas, knives, nunchakus, bo staffs and swords. She could show him a thing or two.

She walked over to the rack and took another sword off the wall. *Shit!* It weighed a ton! No wonder he smirked when she picked it up.

Even though she strained to hold it in both hands, she made sure not to let him know. She would give anything to smack that look right off his face. Instead, she concentrated hard on not dropping the sword. She wouldn't give him the satisfaction. She dared not try to maneuver it as he had.

"A male taught you?" He sounded surprised.

"Yes. Thirteen Earth years of training." Taio laughed and shook his head in disbelief. "It's not unusual on my planet," she said. "A male can teach a female how to fight or even a female can teach a male."

He laughed harder. "There could never be such a thing on my world."

She turned her head away. "I earned a black belt, first Dan in Kyokushin Karate. On Earth I'm considered to be a great fighter."

"Your people did not fare well in the war against the Loconuist. The fighting techniques of your species mean nothing to me." *Ouch.* If the sword in her hands wasn't so heavy, she would have swung it at him. *Asshole.*

"We didn't know how to fight them. We'd never encountered aliens before."

"Then it is good that I will take care of you from now on."

Her head snapped around. "I don't need you to take care of me."

"You were captured by the Loconuist and the Tresdonians almost killed you."

She shrugged. "But they didn't."

He smirked. "Because I saved you."

"Thanks, but I can take care of myself."

"It doesn't matter. You are my responsibility now. You are my slave."

Her eyes, squinting and cold, fixed on his. "Ship told me those assholes on that planet gave me to you. I think you got cheated. I'm not a slave. Not yours or anyone else's."

"If this arrangement does not suit you, I could turn the vessel around and give you back to the Tresdonians." He turned from her and put the heavy sword back on the wall rack.

Her heart began pounding in her chest. He wouldn't...

"No. I'm not going back there." She held her sword tightly in her grasp.

"Then you are my slave." He stalked slowly toward her. His eyes locked on hers.

"No." She backed away from him. *This cannot happen.*

"You are mine." He took another step toward her. "You will need to get used to the idea."

"Never."

Abruptly, Taio turned and walked from the room. She blinked at the empty doorway. The cold surface of the wall was against her back. Without meaning to, she'd backed herself flush up against it. She held the sword close to her chest, shielding her body, her breathing rapid and pulse bounding. She stayed there until her arms shook from the sword's weight.

She was no one's slave.

# Chapter Eight

**ဆ**

"We will dock in Sonis airspace tonight," Ship said.

Her pulse quickened. "Really?"

She was sitting on the edge of the bed in her small cabin, pulling on her shoes. At least the entity waited until she was out of bed and dressed before dropping the news on her. If he had given it to her before, she might have decided to spend the whole day in bed, buried beneath the covers.

"Are you afraid?"

"I'm never afraid."

"Your heart rate and breathing have increased tremendously. It only does that when you are in the presence of Taio."

"Stop reading me!"

Would she ever get any privacy? The entity had been in her presence since she woke up. It wasn't that she didn't like him, because she did. So far, he was her only friend. But he was constant; even when he pretended not to be by her, she still felt his presence.

Eventually he would know her innermost feelings. Although she was sure the entity couldn't tell the difference between fear and arousal, he would figure it out soon enough.

"It is perfectly fine to be scared of the unknown, Eva. You have been through a lot in the past three cycles."

"I know. I just don't want to seem weak."

"There is a lot of talk about you on the vessel, but weak has not been mentioned at all."

*Interesting.*

"Can you tell me what Taio plans to do with me?"

"I am not sure. You will have to ask him directly."

She snorted. "Not in this lifetime." She had not seen him since the day in the training room, avoiding him at all costs.

"I told you before, Taio has never harmed a female. You do not need to be afraid."

"Whatever. I already had a run-in with him. I want to stay as far away from that giant as possible."

"Then I guess we will both learn your fate together. I thought maybe you would want to have some say in it, for a change."

"You are so getting on my nerves." The entity was right, it was time to take control of her destiny. She would just have to suck it up and talk to the giant who both scared her and made her knees weak every time she saw him. "Where can I find him?"

"He is on the bridge. I will tell him to expect a visit from you."

"Thanks, Ship." Putting all fears aside, she made her way to the control room.

The door slid open. There were five males, including Taio, in the room. He sat in the captain's chair. The large room of monitors and lights gave her a moment's pause as she entered. The men didn't pay much attention to her, except for a quick glance her way before returning to their duties. No one yelled for her to leave, so with her head held high and shoulders back, she walked in his direction, nodding to the crew members as she passed them.

She could feel his eyes lingering on her body, making her conscious of how the suit molded to her, how the neckline was too deep and how her nipples reacted by hardening under his gaze. She hated it, she should've been offended by his smoldering looks, but it had the opposite effect on her body.

She stopped in front of him. "King Taio, I wondered —"

"Taio," he said.

"Excuse me?"

"Taio. I prefer to be called Taio." He leaned back in his chair. His soft black leather uniform stretched across his muscles, defining each one.

"Okay. Taio, I wanted to know what you planned to do with me."

"What *should* I do with you?" His eyes roamed slowly up and down her body.

When she felt her pussy lips swell and the wetness between her legs, she stood ramrod straight. She held her ground and pulled back her shoulders. Her body might betray her, but she would never submit to it.

When his eyes finally met hers, she glared at him. "I don't know what you have planned for me, but I'm here to remind you that I'm no one's slave."

His nostrils flared and he took a deep breath. "Interesting, because I have your ownership paperwork. I was not even expecting to get any, but I can only guess that since you were nothing but trouble for the Tresdonians, they wanted a record of you leaving their possession."

"I don't care what 'paperwork' you have." She took two steps closer to him. "I already warned you."

"Warned me?" Instantly he straightened in his chair. "Do you hear, guards?" he yelled. "The female has 'warned' me."

All of the guards erupted in laughter.

"Asshole." Why did she even bother trying to talk to him? It was all Ship's stupid idea. She turned around to walk away.

Growling low, he reached out and grabbed the back of her suit, yanking her onto his lap. Caught off guard, she struggled. He threw an arm over her stomach and tightened his grip, pinning her in place.

"You will not leave unless I dismiss you," he said. He growled deep in his chest.

She bucked and wiggled against his grasp. Her neckline stretched low across her breasts. "You don't own me!"

"I will...in every way." Taio inhaled deeply. "I can smell how much you want me."

"Let me go, you Neanderthal!"

Her bun unraveled as she banged her head on his chest.

"I like the view from up here."

"Let. Go. Of. Me."

He instantly stiffened. Noticing the change in him, she stilled as well. She followed his gaze to find it resting on her naked breast. It had sprung free during their struggle. *Oh shit.*

"Leave us." His voice was deep and possessive.

"Let me cover myself at least," she whispered. Her hands gripped his forearm, her nails digging into his flesh.

Only after the last person exited the room did he release her. She shot up and adjusted herself with her back to him.

"You embarrassed me," she said. She worked at righting her suit.

"I am not concerned about your embarrassment. You came onto my bridge and challenged me in front of my guards."

"It wasn't meant to be a challenge." She turned around, her face reddening. "I wanted to know your plans. Can't I just live out a normal life? Do my own thing?"

"I am not in the habit of acquiring beings of different species and taking them to my home to 'do their own thing'."

For the briefest moment, they stared at each other. They were at a standstill. Her fists balled at her sides. Her eyes fixed on the tattoo on his face. This was the first time she had seen his tattoo up close.

"What is that a picture of?" The words escaped her lips before she could stop herself.

She thought he wasn't going to answer as he ran his hand over the claw on his face.

"It is a *varitizar*." His hands caressed the talons surrounding his eye.

"How did you get it? It looks like some kind of tribal marking." Everyone on the vessel had a facial tattoo of some type or another.

"When males come of age, we go through a ritual called an enlightenment ceremony. We become warriors. During the ceremony, our animal guides reveal themselves to us. In my case, it was the *varitizar*."

"Is it as bad as it looks?" She extended her hand to touch his face. Then, realizing what she was doing, she pulled back. *Mess with fire and you will get burned.*

"Worse." A sinister smile graced his lips.

"What about the females? Do they participate in the ceremony?"

"Never."

"Why not?"

"Because it is unheard of." He raised his eyebrow. "Do you want to see the rest of it?"

She nodded and he pulled his shirt over his head in one swift movement, revealing a perfectly chiseled torso. Her eyes roamed over the elaborate tattoo of a red and blue beast.

Its head spanned one side of his chest. It had yellow eyes and oversized fangs too big to fit in its ugly mouth. The body extended down into his pants and wrapped around to his back. One of the arms extended to the other side of his chest, with the claw resting right above his heart. The other arm snaked up the side of his face with the claw holding his eye.

"Besides, females are not warriors. They are good for other things on my world, and right now I am more interested in *those* things." He spread his legs wider, revealing a massive hard-on.

It wasn't as if she hadn't fantasized about it. Hell, every time she looked at him, she had naughty thoughts of running her tongue down his body. Who wouldn't? The man was built for sex. Well, fighting and sex. Her body pulsated, wet with just the thought of him spreading her legs and plunging between them.

He grabbed the front of her suit and pulled her close to him again. This time she didn't resist. Settling her between his legs, he reached for her zipper, slowly working it to her waist.

With both her breasts finally free, he slid her arms out of the suit. *Shit.* She should really stop him. Really, she should. If she could just get her hands to comply and push him away or at least get her mouth to obey her and tell him to stop, she would.

Positioned between his legs, she should turn away and leave. But her feet wouldn't obey her screaming mind either. Her body was putty in his hands. Funny, she thought. When she had thought of Taio trying to rape her, she envisioned kicking his ass and sending him to the healing bay.

But since this didn't border on rape, there was no Plan B.

# Chapter Nine

## ❧

A hot mouth on her rib cage jolted her from her thoughts. Taio was tracing her ribs with his tongue and damn did it feel good. Too damn good. Eva inhaled and fluttered her eyes closed.

"I can smell your musk." Taio's voice was a hard whisper. "Your body is calling to me." His tongue found its way to the underside of her breast and then trailed to her plump, hard nipple.

She brought her hands up and gripped his shoulders.

"Don't try to fight me," he said.

She let out a ragged breath and he devoured her entire nipple, pulling it into his mouth and gently sucking it.

Her hands moved to cradle the back of his head, drawing his hot mouth closer and harder to her breast. Taio's deep groan rippled off her breast. Eva raked her nails across his scalp as his lips and tongue teased the erect nipple. Through heavy eyelids, she watched as he concentrated on sucking her nipple, his eyes closed, his hands holding her waist.

Taio's teeth nibbled and then moved to do the same to the other one. Eva moaned, grabbing him tighter, arching her back to meet his mouth.

She needed more, her body melting into him. She murmured as he dipped an oversized hand inside her jumpsuit. His fingers slid between her moist folds, seeking out her wet treasure. Slipping over her small nub, he hovered there and stroked. Eva held on tighter and opened her legs wider, giving him all access.

"What is this?" Her clit throbbed and pulsed under his touch.

"A clit," she replied breathlessly.

His calloused finger slowly rubbed and stroked. Her legs started to weaken from underneath her. *Oh shit.*

"This feels good to you?"

"Yes."

She was falling apart around him. His finger rubbed painfully slow on her clit while he used his other hand to lower her body to the ground. She melted to the floor without resistance.

"If I had known you were going to be this compliant, I would have woken you up rubbing on this."

Once lowered, he stopped only to slide the jumpsuit down her legs. She lay naked before him, wondering how different she was from females on his world. His lavender eyes turned a shade darker as he hungrily watched her. Groaning, he took her by the ankles and spread them wide. Whatever embarrassment she had quickly disappeared as he leaned forward and brought her clit into his hot mouth.

*Oh my!* A moan passed over her lips and her back arched high.

Taio sucked and licked, taking his time, enjoying his newfound toy. With every tug and caress, her eyes rolled to the back of her head. Reaching down, she grabbed at his hair, grinding on his face.

Growling, he dipped his tongue deep into her pussy. He lapped at the liquid there, finally replacing his tongue with a large finger.

Her hips instinctively pumped against the finger that slid in and out of her wet sheath. It had been too long since she had been touched as he was touching her now. Her core tightened and contracted around his finger. Her stomach knotted as he lowered his mouth, covering her pearl again, expertly licking, sucking and fingering her.

She moaned and bucked against him. "Please, Taio, please. I need you now."

He ignored her plea, choosing instead to continue his probe. Eva couldn't take anymore, she needed him now. She clawed at his hair and shoulders, trying to lift him.

Taio sat back on his heels, eyes focused on her throbbing channel. She was dripping and waiting.

His hand hooked in the front of his pants, tugging them down. Displayed before her was the most beautiful sight she had ever seen. The tattoo didn't stop at his torso— one leg of the beast stretched down Taio's leg. Her eyes followed the path of the other leg and widened as they rested on his long, thick shaft. The beast had its claw wrapped around the wide base.

Eva gasped as it aimed right at her. The size! It was huge! He was definitely in proportion with the rest of his body. There was absolutely no way she would be able to take it all.

"You faced two Tresdonians, but you are scared of this." Taio grasped his thick cock in his hand.

"I'm not scared of anything." She licked her lips. Her mouth salivated as she anticipated her mouth around it.

"Next time, little one." He chuckled. "I have to finish what I started."

"Don't call me that."

He raised his eyebrow.

"Someone else used to call me that."

He grabbed her feet and opened her legs wider. "Right now I am the only thought you should have."

Heat radiated from her pussy as he moved to hover over her, nestling himself between her legs. Taio pressed the tip of his oversized head to her small, wet opening.

Eva tried adjusting herself under him. He weighed more than she thought. She wanted him bad, but she didn't want to be crushed in the meantime. Taio paused before rolling onto his back, taking her with him.

"I would not want to injure you." Taio smacked the hard floor with his hand.

Eva rose and planted both feet firmly on the floor. With her hair streaming around her, she squatted above him. Her hand trembled as she reached down, grabbed his cock and positioned it to her tight opening.

She hesitated. She really wasn't afraid of the size or the man, but what this would mean for her future.

Taio caressed her thighs, urging her down. Taking a deep breath, Eva slowly lowered. The head pressed against her tightness, not budging, too big to enter her. Determined, she tried to work it in, wiggling onto it.

His fingers tightened on her thighs. "If you keep that up, you will make me spill my seed." Taio pumped up in a hard thrust. The large head penetrated her.

She closed her eyes and threw her head back. "Oh fuck!"

Taio grabbed both thighs, holding her unsteady body while he thrust his hips up and down, inching his thick cock deeper into her tight sheath. Her slick walls coated him as it stretched her open.

She slowly moved her hips to meet his rhythm, taking more of him, inch by glorious inch, pumping the length of his penetrating shaft.

Taio's hands moved to grip her hips. With the pain receding, Eva was soon overcome by pleasure. Her pace slightly quickened. He filled her up and she wanted more.

The sounds of his shaft now slickened by her juices filled the bridge. Moaning, she dropped to her knees. His shaft filled her to the core, completely stretching her to the limits.

With a groan, Taio rolled his eyes back into his head. "Great Ancients."

His fingers dug painfully into her skin. She rocked on his shaft, increasing her pace. Each time she rose, her pussy milked him, sucking him back in.

He grabbed her tighter and pumped her faster and harder. Her breasts bounced and swayed in his face. He took one of the hard nipples in his mouth and sucked. His teeth grazed against her sensitive bud.

She slammed her hips down on him. Any fears she had before were long since gone, replaced by intense need.

"You are mine," he groaned.

Eva erupted with a scream, her walls contracting and spasming against his rod. Holding her tight against his body, he thrust up, spilling his seed deep inside her.

Spent, they both lay quietly, breathing hard, trying to catch their breaths. Eva tried sliding off him but was stopped short by a firm hand. Taio's cock thickened and pulsed inside her again.

"Again?"

Taio answered by pumping his thick shaft in her swollen sheath. Sore, but wanting more, she rose to her knees and elbows. Her hair fanned across his chest. His fingers dug into her hips, holding her in place as he pumped fast and hard.

She would surely have trouble walking but didn't care. Never before had she felt anything as good as this.

After they were done, Taio carried her back to her quarters. Feeling the soft cushion of her bed, Eva curled in a ball.

"This doesn't mean that you own me," she said groggily.

"You are already mine."

# Chapter Ten

ဆ

Eva readied herself as best she could. She stood at the airlock with the crew. Taio flanked her on the right and Rasha on the left. Although she wasn't tethered to either one of them, with their bodies pressed up against hers, she had the distinct feeling she was supposed to stay at their side.

Taio hadn't mentioned their tryst on the bridge. Had she expected him to? Maybe a "How are you feeling?" or "Was it as good for you as it was for me?" To the first question, her muscles were a little sore and she was surprised she could even walk straight. And yes, it was the best sex she ever had.

She was sure he enjoyed himself as well. The "love bites" on her breasts, torso, hips and legs still throbbed. She glanced quickly at him, wondering if the scratches she raked down his chest were still there or if he took a trip to the healing bay. *Damn.* She should have gone there too, she thought, not wanting to be the only one still marked up.

She straightened her back and squared her shoulders, intent on projecting some resemblance of confidence, even though the unknown world scared her shitless. Parading through enough orphanages, group homes and foster homes had taught her that the first impression was a lasting one. If the males standing by her side were any indication of the size of the people she would encounter, she would surely be one of the smallest here. A good first impression was vital.

The airlock opened, releasing a cool gust of wind that swept across her body.

"Here I go," she muttered. Taking a deep breath, she walked beside Taio and Rasha as they led the way down a stark white corridor.

To her credit, only after reaching the central common area did she falter slightly, stumbling over her own feet. Taio wrapped his calloused hand around her elbow, offering support. She yanked her arm away. The last thing she needed was to appear weak in the eyes of his people. He chuckled softly at her side. She glared at him; of course someone in his position wouldn't know the ill effects of a bad first impression.

"Very well, little one." He smirked.

"Stop calling me that. I'm not a child."

"I can attest to that." His voice was no more than a low, honeyed tone.

With a little prayer under her breath, she entered the colorful common room.

She froze in the entryway, forcing everyone to go around her. Transfixed in her spot, she looked around the room in amazement, her eyes trying to take in all of her new surroundings at once. "Beautiful."

Taio stopped at her side. "I'm glad you approve."

Wide-eyed, she looked at deep-red walls with blue-patterned designs. The moldings that framed the ceiling and entryways were intricately made out of what appeared to be blue blown glass. Oversized chairs were strategically placed around the room, framing the three fireplaces. With another breath, she stepped deeper into the room and watched as the crew was greeted by numerous people. She had little choice but to assume the greeters were family members welcoming home their loved ones.

*I can get through this.* The thought washed over her mind as she stood still with her eyes focused ahead. The melee of people continued to bustle around her with exchanges of love she could now understand with the help of her fully functioning Universal Translator.

This wasn't anything she couldn't deal with. She had been in situations the same as this before, many times; loved ones welcoming each other at the airport, parents greeting classmates after school plays and surrounding the martial artist fighter after a big win.

Although this was a different planet, the logistics were still the same. From experience, she knew how to stay motionless so that no one would notice her, wouldn't notice no one was coming to welcome her. And if no one saw, then they wouldn't pity her.

As she blocked out the voices around her, the familiar feeling of overwhelming isolation slowly crept up on her. *Get a grip.* She shook her head slightly, trying to remove the cancerous thought that, if left unchecked, would consume her. Once the crowd died down, she could figure out where she belonged and go to that place.

A tall golden-skinned female walked over to Taio. "Take her with you," he said. Eva remained rooted in place, her eyes fixed ahead.

"Eva, this is Mazel, my personal assistant. Go with her." Taio gently nudged her toward the stranger.

Too relieved to object, she followed the female as she led her through the maze of halls. Eva rushed to take two steps for every one step the long-legged female took. Mazel didn't slow her pace to allow for her to catch up. Eva spent a great deal of the tour watching her back. When Mazel turned around to reprimand her for not keeping up, Eva noticed that her severe bangs were cut high above light-green eyes that slanted, reminding her of someone of Asian descent.

Eva followed Mazel through halls lined with framed pictures of scenery that she didn't recognize. She passed by blown-glass vases on carved pedestals. To her, the air of expense clung to every item. Eva held her head high as she passed onlookers in the hallway, all with surprised glances cast her way, murmuring and whispering under their breaths. She straightened her shoulders as well. This had the same feeling as being the new girl in school, but with a new girl on the planet kind of twist.

Only after Mazel pointed to a door and explained that it led to the training field did Eva decide to pay attention to her guide. She would need to find her way back there.

She had feigned remote interest as Mazel explained where to find the kitchens, the healing center and other common areas. Mazel led her through a foyer that opened to an entryway with two guards. The guards looked just as intimidating as the ones from Taio's vessel. Mazel passed them with a short nod of the head. Eva followed close on her heels, doing much the same.

She couldn't help but turn around to take a quick peek at the guards, wondering if they were going to follow them to wherever their destination was.

"Humph." Eva slammed into Mazel's back, then retreated two steps. The female slowly turned around to give Eva another disapproving stare. "Sorry."

"Watch where you walk. You are too small to be so careless. I'm sure you're just as fragile as you appear."

"I'm not fragile." The beating she took from the Tresdonians proved as much.

Mazel held out her hand. When Eva stared at it blankly, the other woman reached for her. Eva took a quick step back. "I need to scan your hand for the security system."

"Oh." She placed her palm in Mazel's hand.

It took only two seconds for her to be registered with the door security. The light on the panel flashed green and the door unlocked with a click. Mazel pushed the door open and ushered her into what appeared to be, well, a royal palace within a palace.

She was completely blown away. The beauty within his palace she had seen so far had been magnified tenfold in his private suite. The main living area was filled with oversized and overstuffed pillows in an array of colors and the walls had the same multicolored theme.

The artwork that hung there was of animals she wished never to encounter in her lifetime. The smell in the air reminded her of Taio. His scent clung to the furniture. The overstuffed couches and chairs were so large, she felt they would swallow her up.

She kept up with Mazel as she showed her to the kitchen that was more elaborate than the dining hall on the *Saia II*. Mazel gave her instructions on how to use the console in the wall where she would order food.

Eva moved closer to read the menu. *Filbaster meat sandwich. Yuck.* Her nose wrinkled in disgust. The thought of eating made her already queasy stomach flop uncomfortably.

Her mind was officially overloaded. She blew out a breath. She definitely wasn't on Earth anymore.

But nothing prepared her for what Mazel showed her next from a high balcony. Standing on the balcony, she caught her first glimpse of the spectacular view. On the distant horizon were two setting suns. One was larger than the other, bathing the sky in a dim orange light.

"Beautiful," she whispered.

Never had she seen an alien sky. It truly took her breath away.

"I have been to many other planets and this is by far the best sunset there is to behold," Mazel said, her eyes fixed on the sky. Eva tensed when Mazel moved to stand next to her by the railing. So far, Mazel had acted as though showing her around had been more of a chore than anything else.

"You should have Taio tell you their story one day." Mazel nodded to the suns, her face softening.

"They have a story?" Eva asked, relaxing.

"Yes, a very interesting one. But I think it is one our king would prefer to tell you himself." She turned away and walked toward the door.

Turning to join her, Eva spotted a large tan planet on the other side of the horizon.

"What is that?" she asked.

"That is Drazlan. The home planet," Mazel said. Her eyes trained on the not-so-distant planet.

Eva looked past Drazlan, seeing millions of twinkling lights that lit up the sky. Constellations that were unfamiliar to her. The realization hit her. No matter how far she looked, she would not see Earth. Her home was in a distant past, millions of light-years away from where she currently stood.

"Come, let me show you to your room." Mazel's voice pulled her back to Sonis. Before turning, her eyes caught the sight of greenery at the bottom of the stairs that led to the private royal gardens. Tomorrow, she would venture onto the private grounds to feel dirt and grass underneath her feet once again. Tomorrow, because at the moment, the confidence to venture out into the eerie and unknown dark world eluded her.

Instead, she let Mazel lead her up the stairs where she assumed her room would be. The servant's quarters crossed her mind. She'd be happy if they were half as impressive as the rooms she passed through. Her stomach lurched. A slave, the idea would never settle with her.

With each step, her lead-filled legs became heavier and heavier. The emotions of the day weighing her down, she hoped for a soft bed. Her bed on the Loconuist spacecraft consisted of nothing more than a meager pallet. The *Saia II* had offered her a step up, a bed intended for a seven- to eight-foot male, with nothing but a thin mattress between her back and the metal frame.

She followed her guide into a room that was two times bigger than her entire apartment in Ann Arbor. The room held a bed and little else. From what she could make out, the room was occupied. Although the room was immaculate, the various swords on the walls and the heavy scent of musk filling the air were a dead giveaway. She was in a male-occupied room.

Eva froze in place and looked around. "I think there might be a mistake."

"No, Taio has instructed me to bring you to his private rooms."

"I don't think you understand." Eva's eyes darted around the room. "Did Taio tell you that I'm his slave?" she whispered, although they were alone in the room. The last thing she wanted was to be humiliated by Taio dragging her out of his bed in the middle of the night.

Mazel scoffed and smiled. "He told me this is where you will sleep." Mazel walked toward an open door. "Ship has provided me with your size."

Eva followed her to what appeared to be a closet and peeked inside. There were rows of women's clothing, not much different than the colorful, long, flowing gown Mazel wore. Mazel selected a bundle of material from a shelf. Walking past Eva, she laid it on the bed.

"Are you sure he wants me to stay in here? Where is he going to sleep?"

Mazel raised one thick, dark eyebrow at her.

"Oh. Well. Okay."

After wishing her a good night, Mazel left the room.

All alone, Eva sat on the large bed next to the long, transparent gown Mazel had laid across it. Reaching over, she let her hands run over the gown. The material, albeit see-through, was beautiful and soft to the touch. She picked it up, amazed at how light and airy the gown was. It could have been something right out of a Victoria's Secret catalogue.

What did he want from her? Why would he want her in his private quarters?

Well, she could understand he wanted to continue a physical relationship. She briefly thought back to the afternoon on the bridge. The sex had been more than amazing. But to live in his private quarters? Now that was moving a bit fast.

She had spent her entire life being independent and able to provide for herself. Now she was not only a slave, but would have to share her personal space with a stranger. *This will be different,* she thought. Could she ever get used to her new circumstances? Living as a slave, a sex slave, a concubine?

She'd been in one committed relationship in her life, with Alan. He had been everything she thought she wanted and needed in a man. They met while he was in residency at the hospital where she worked.

Of course she fell in love with him right away. Who wouldn't? He was tall and handsome, blond hair and blue eyes. Being a doctor definitely didn't hurt.

Unfortunately, she found out the hard way his feelings had not been the same. He had seen her as a way to pass the time, a nice "diversion", he had told her. A diversion that lasted two years? She had broken his nose when he told her that. There was no way she was falling that hard for anyone ever again.

*I have to set Taio straight.*

Peeling off her clothes and kicking out of her boots, she made her way back to the closet. She would find her own pajamas, thank you very much. Something less see-through. Selecting one of Taio's shirts, she pulled it over her head. Yawning and slipping under the array of large blankets, she drifted to sleep.

*Tomorrow. I'll set him straight tomorrow.*

# Chapter Eleven

ജ

Eva's body sank into the plush bed. She imagined that the mattress was stuffed with a million feathers. She didn't want to move. She could stay here forever, she thought, as she relaxed deeper under the blankets. She sighed as she thought of the only downside of the moment, the stab of pain in her ribs.

Taio had one arm thrown across her body and the other was sandwiched between her ribs and the comfy bed. She moved to readjust her position for the fiftieth time. Those times, just as this one, she was met with resistance. Taio grunted and pulled her closer to him. Even in his sleep, Taio thought he owned her.

He had her securely snuggled to his warm, muscular body. Not a bad place to be if it weren't for the pain. Taio snored lightly. His breath came out in hot puffs on the top of her head. Tendrils of hair blew lightly with each exhalation. If she wasn't a nervous wreck, she might have enjoyed the peaceful moment.

She was on an alien planet being held hostage by an alien king who, by the way, thought she was his slave. She was the only human here. There was no possible escape. Even if she wanted to escape, where would she go? Eva let out a hard breath, finally coming to the conclusion that she had to make the best of it. Taio stirred and pulled her closer, as if he sensed she was thinking of an escape.

She was trapped. She wouldn't be able to escape from Sonis, let alone get out of bed, until after Taio woke up.

Her only reprieve was the large window that took up the entire side of one wall. She watched as the suns rose, illuminating the darkened sky. The light breeze coming through the window caused the long, pale-yellow sheer curtains to open and close with every small gust. With daylight, she could clearly see Drazlan in the distance.

Every so often, a winged creature squawked as it passed the window. Calling the thing a bird would be a far stretch. On the third pass by the window, the creature landed on the table that sat outside on the balcony.

Its face looked more human than bird. It had lips instead of a beak. Short, stocky legs supported a plump body. Its green feathers were billowy and fluffy. Eva shuddered under Taio's arms and snuggled closer. If those creatures soared through the skies, she was afraid to find out how the creatures walking on the ground looked.

Taio moaned as her butt pressed firmly against his hardening cock.

"This is a nice way to start the day," he said, his voice deep and groggy.

"Argh."

"Not a morning person, I take it?" Taio laughed. His chest vibrated against her back. His cock, now fully erect, pressed against her backside.

"Since this is the first real morning I've had in three years, err, cycles, I can honestly say that I don't know anymore."

Taio kissed her on the back of her head. "Then we have to change that, don't we?" His hands reached for her breasts, palming them through the rough material of the shirt. The material against her nipples felt good. Too good. Taio playfully squeezed and plucked at each sensitive bud.

She wanted the memories of the last years wiped out. She hadn't seen a sun rise or set in so long. It was time to start anew. She pressed her butt closer to his cock, grinding in slow circular motions. The feel of hot skin penetrated the shirt, her eyes closing as she realized he was entirely naked. If she had known that, she would have gotten this party started hours ago.

Taio reached down and lifted her leg over his. While one hand leisurely massaged a breast, the other rubbed her clit.

"Did you sleep well?" he asked.

"Yes." She twirled her hips again. "But I'm starting to really enjoy my morning better."

"I aim to please." Taio dipped a large finger in her wet pussy. Eva raked her nails across his thighs. "We can do this every morning."

Eva tugged the shirt over her hips. Taio's shaft nestled hot against the crack of her ass. "Where am I going to stay while I'm here?"

Taio grabbed her hips, lifting her off the bed to slide his cock between her legs. "What do you mean by 'while you are here'? This is your home now."

Eva slid her slick heat along his shaft, shuddering as the hard ridge of the head pressed over her clit. Reaching between her legs, she pressed it against her. She pushed back, trying to force the large head to breach her small opening. It didn't work. Taio held her hips firmly in place and pushed up hard. Eva gasped as the head filled her sore and swollen sheath, stretching her painfully.

Taking his time, Taio slowly moved in and out, letting her adjust to his thickness. The pain subsided with each slow thrust. She buried her head in the pillows, panting as pleasure overrode all her senses.

As her moans were muffled by the pillow, Taio's deep moans filled the room. She wrapped her arms around the pillow as his speed quickened and his thrusts became harder. Holding her in place, Taio pumped deeper, his hips slapping against her ass. She cried out as his cock stretched her to the max.

Just when she thought she would split in two, Taio thrust deeper with a roar. The feel of his hot liquid spurting and coating her walls was enough to send her over the edge. Her walls contracted as her climax met his.

Taio rolled onto his back and positioned her to lie on his sweaty chest. His dark, damp chest hairs pressed against her cheek as she made circular patterns in them with her fingers.

"Exactly how far away from Earth are we?"

"Eva, it doesn't matter." He stroked a hand through her hair. "The Loconuist are there, it's not safe, you can never return."

Eva closed her eyes against the mental blow. "I miss it."

"Tell me, what do you miss most?"

*Everything.* "For starters, music. I miss music. I would give anything to hear *Drinks Up* by A.O. Or even log onto the Internet to catch the latest Orangey and Purple webisode."

"I do not know what 'the Internet' is, but we do have music. Some of the best musicians have traveled over great distances to perform on Sonis."

She rolled her eyes, doubting they would have Afro-Punk on Sonis. "It won't be the same."

"In time, you will learn to call Sonis home."

"Don't sound so confident, 'master'. I'm a slave here. It can never be home," she mumbled. "But what I miss most is Ally."

"She is your family?"

She shook her head. "I joined up with Ally and her husband, Jim, during the invasion. But we became family in the short time that we were hiding from the aliens. Jim died before we were captured. Ally and I watched over each other on the spacecraft."

He kissed her on the top of her head and gave her arm a reassuring squeeze. "Eva, the odds of finding her are not in your favor."

"I know, Ship told me. But he also promised to help me look for her."

"Ship will do his best to keep his promise."

For a moment she lay in silence, wondering how Ally was faring. What kind of person she had been sold to, if she was a slave as well. Her head popped up. "What about some kind of slave buy-back program?"

Taio frowned. "You are mine, to keep. You'll stay here with me." Taio's arm gripped her tighter.

She rested her head back on his muscled chest. "Taio, I'm not slave material. Even though I was given to you, I still think I should have the opportunity to buy my freedom. I could work for it."

"You have a job." He flicked a finger across her nipple.

"No, a real job. A job so I can pay you back." She pinched his nipple in return.

"This is the only job you need. I plan to keep you very busy." He rubbed her leg and gave it a playful pat.

"What about training your guards? I could help with that."

Taio laughed. "As I told you before, males and females do not train together. You will not find a female training on Sonis at all. That is not their place."

She lifted her head to stare at him. "I could change that."

"A female's place is not on the training field. She is expected to clean, cook, serve or attend to the children." He waved his free hand in the air as he talked. "Oh, or she can serve as a personal assistant to a male."

"The same as Mazel?"

"Yes, Mazel has served me for a very long time."

Eva squinted, wondering just how well she served him.

Taio laughed. "Not in the capacity you are thinking, little one."

"What about Rasha? Does he have one too?" She lowered her head back on his chest. The hairs tickled her ear and cheek, but she nuzzled into them anyway.

"Rasha is between assistants right now. But that position is not for you. I already told you what your job will be."

And if he had it his way, she would be doing her "job" all day, every day. Sheesh, their combined juices were still leaking out of her. *Oh shit!* She squeezed her eyes shut.

"Umm...Taio? Do you have anything here to prevent pregnancy?" Shit, shit, shit, she mentally kicked herself. Birth control hadn't been on her mind in a very long time. This was a fine time to remember it, *after* the fact.

"We welcome every pregnancy that occurs on Sonis. But if you are wondering about yourself, do not. My race has never been able to procreate with other species beside our own."

"Oh. Okay." Her heart slowed to its regular pace. At least she didn't have to worry about that while she was here.

*Hmm...no kids, ever.*

She shook her head. No need to think or worry about children. She needed him to give her some measure of independence.

"Taio, I want a job. I mean, I've worked since I was fourteen years old. I have to be able to provide for myself."

"A Sonis female is not burdened with such things. Either her mate is expected to provide for her or she remains the responsibility of her father until she does mate."

"I don't mind being burdened by working, really. My first job was mopping floors at the local ice cream parlor."

"Is that what you did before you were taken from Earth?"

Eva choked. "Oh God no. Believe it or not, I actually moved up in the world. I have a bachelor's degree in nursing and worked at a hospital, a health facility, as a registered nurse...umm, healer."

"You had more jobs than one?"

Eva laughed. "Yes. On Earth, we worked. Men, women and children."

"Then you should feel privileged that I have brought you to Sonis. Your only responsibility will be to take care of me." She could feel his chest puff out under her head.

"Taio..."

"Eva, you are mine, that part is nonnegotiable. But I can assure you that I will never treat you as a slave."

Eva lifted to her hands to stare down at him, her hair framing her face and draping his chest.

"How do you get the other slaves acclimated into this society? Were they born slaves or were they forced into it?"

"To be honest, we don't have slaves on Sonis." He cleared his throat and looked away. "You, ah, are the first one."

She punched him in the chest. "You have got to be kidding! I'm the only slave on this entire rock!"

"Yes."

Eva threw herself onto her back and pulled the cover up to her neck. Taio reached to pull the cover down, but she slapped his hand out of the way.

"So there has got to be room for negotiation. If I can't work for my freedom, I can do something else. And no, sex doesn't count."

She was the only slave? Really? No wonder everyone stared at her last night. She was the only freaking slave here!

"The head of your household, your father, would negotiate your terms. Since he is not here, as your owner, I would serve in his place and I reject the terms." Taio shrugged, as if he had the problem solved.

"I have to figure out how to spend my time here. I can't sit around waiting for you to get hard." Just then, a thought hit her. "Can I work for you? Ship mentioned something about a business?"

"Eva, my businesses aren't accommodating for females."

"Businesses?"

"I have Sonis Mercenary, which is run by my younger brother Kiehle. I haven't participated in the day-to-day operations of that company for over ten cycles. Then there is Sonis Gold. We mine for gold and sell it throughout the galaxy. Neither business is suitable for a female."

"So those are out." She crossed her arms over her breasts. "I can tell you now, I'm not kitchen or cleaning material. And while we're on that subject, I saw the clothes in the closet. Thanks, but I'm going to need something less...girly."

"Eva, the female clothes are traditional Sonis dress. I can't allow you to dress as a male."

"Tsk, tsk, tsk." She waved a finger at him. "We are negotiating."

"And I told you, I do not negotiate with females."

"An exception has to be made because I don't have a father. I've been negotiating for myself since I was emancipated at sixteen. I think I can handle this."

"What do you mean? The fathers of Earth did not make decisions for their female children?"

"It's not that. I'm an orphan." Taio crumpled his brow in confusion. "I didn't have a mother or father. I lived in an orphanage."

"I don't understand."

"It's a place where children go if they don't have a mother or father to take care of them."

"But—"

"But that's not what we're negotiating. I want to be able to wear the same kind of clothes that I wore on the vessel. I think it's only fair. I gave up the idea of working, now it's your turn to give me something in return."

He was silent in thought for a moment. "Okay, you can keep your clothes. I'm not sure how the other females will react to such a thing. A female in males' clothing." He shook his head in disbelief.

"They'll get over it."

It didn't take her long to figure out Taio was right. The females on Sonis didn't want anything to do with her. She waved and smiled as she passed them in the halls. Instead of a return gesture, everyone averted their eyes and pretended she didn't exist.

Mazel even tried to help out, but not even her teaching of "Sonis" ways did anything to get the other women to open up to her. The males avoided her, but she expected Taio had a hand in that. But to be ostracized by the females was unexpected to say the least.

Could they all be this hung up about clothes? If wearing gowns was a requirement for friends, she decided to resign herself to being alone.

# Chapter Twelve

## ഔ

The past week had been nothing but a test of wills. Apparently Mazel hadn't gotten Taio's memo about the clothes. That woman didn't take no for an answer.

Every morning, Mazel laid out a gown, prodding her to wear it, trying to make her a "proper" Sonis female. Eva was not a dress kind of girl. She was a jeans and t-shirt or scrubs kind of girl. And if Mazel wasn't bad enough, Taio imposed one rule after another.

Eva sat on the grass-covered ground, the suns' rays beating down on her back as she watched the sandy field fifty yards in front of her. A protective covering was flung haphazardly across her head and shoulders. She had strict orders to keep the covering on at all times; otherwise, Taio would not have let her come back out into the suns.

The covering wasn't heavy or cumbersome; it just made her stand out as...different. No one else she'd encountered so far had to wear a sun blanket. But no one she encountered had sunburned shoulders, arms and face either.

She scoffed when he first told her — no, commanded — she wear it at all times while she was outdoors. She couldn't get skin cancer in a couple of days, and besides, all she would need to do was take a quick trip to the healing bay to be cured. Taio hadn't found the humor in that. He didn't stand down and neither did she.

The first time she had tried to leave the palace, she found that Ship had created some kind of force field around all the exits that wouldn't let her through. By heavens, they intended to trap her indoors with an invisible shield that stopped only her.

It pissed her off, but secretly she admired their *Star Trek* kind of technology. Threatening Ship did nothing to bring down the shield. She was finally forced to go back to her room and retrieve the blanket. Ship was officially on her shit list now.

She would think about plotting her revenge on Ship later, but right now she was wondering if she scooted up a couple more feet, would the guards on the field notice her. So far, Taio felt strongly about two things, the protective sun blanket and the training field. *Well, technically, I'm not on the training field.*

Since the first day of finding it, she couldn't stay away from the excitement this place held for her. She understood why he was worried for her. The men were gigantic and the weapons were unfamiliar. Fighting! She clenched and unclenched her fists under the blanket. She wanted to hit something.

*Hard.*

For the past four days, she had come out to the training field, and each time had inched a few feet closer. The men didn't seem to notice her proximity. She just hoped Taio would also be oblivious to her pursuit as well.

A group of guards practiced with the *jango*, a fighting sword that had almost the size and look of a javelin. She wished she had one herself to hold and practice with. She sat mesmerized as the guards swung the body-length, metallic weapon with ease. The suns' rays reflected off them, creating a spectacular light show.

"Wow. This is great."

Eva looked up to see a female with pale-pink skin, short, hot-pink spiky hair and coal-black eyes staring down at her. Eva blinked back her surprise. Where had this chick come from?

"I'm Lo'Ren." The pink female plopped down next to her.

"I'm Eva." The female's arm brushed against her own. Eva scooted over.

"Ohh, royal guards." Lo'Ren looked toward the guards training on the field. "I don't know about you, but the sight of their glistening bodies always makes me think of all the wicked things I can let them do to me."

"Umm, so, you came to watch them train too? I thought I was the only female who came out here."

"I came to sit with you. I've never been out here before. The royal guards are an added bonus." Lo'Ren smiled and winked.

"Sit with me? Why? Wait. Did Taio send you?"

"Yes. My job is to be your friend." Lo'Ren smacked her on her back.

"I'm good. I don't need you to follow me around." Eva closed her eyes and muttered under her breath. "How embarrassing, now he's finding me friends."

"Don't worry. He didn't make me, I volunteered for the job."

Eva groaned. "He asked for volunteers? How many volunteered for the job?"

Lo'Ren laughed.

Eva opened her eyes. "That bad, huh?"

"I was the only one."

Eva groaned again.

"But I wanted to." Lo'Ren cut her eyes sheepishly at Eva. "Anything to get out of cleaning duty."

Eva laughed. "Something tells me you aren't from Sonis."

"It must be the hair." Lo'Ren ran a hand across her pink mane. "Born and raised in Briel, a small work colony in the Lintag asteroid belt."

"Wait. You grew up in an asteroid belt?"

"Briel's finest at your service." Lo'Ren pinched the tips to make her hair stand up even more.

"I didn't know anyone could live in an asteroid belt." Eva turned back to the field. A month ago, she didn't know anyone could live on a moon either. "What are you doing on Sonis? Were you forced to come here?"

"No, no, no. I came on my own. Sonis is supposed to be a growing settlement. Maybe in about three...five...ten cycles." Lo'Ren looked around at the almost barren landscape. "Speaking of my employer, here he comes."

Eva glared at Taio as he walked to her.

"What are you and your new friend doing?" He smiled down on her.

Lo'Ren smiled back. "Feasting our eyes on royal guards."

Taio's smiled dropped to a frown and Eva rolled her eyes. That was what the lout got. Maybe next time he wouldn't pick friends for her who volunteered for the job.

"I like those fighting things they have. Look at all the pretty colors," Lo'Ren said.

"I could have one made for you if you like," Taio said.

"I don't want one. I just like watching the guards with them." Eva and Taio both turned to look at Lo'Ren. "Oh not talking to me."

"You could?" Eva squinted as she looked up at him, the suns at his back.

"I could, if it would keep you from sneaking closer to my training field." He crossed his arms over his chest and stared down at her.

"But Taio, the men don't even mind I'm here. Why can't I train with them? I told you, on my planet, men and women trained side by side all the time.

Of course, males and females didn't train side by side all over Earth, but right now she didn't want to get into specifics about training with him.

"And I have told you, these are not 'men', but warriors. Warriors training with females is not a tradition we practice here."

"Sonis is a new colony, you are still forming your own traditions."

He thought on it for a moment, looking at his guards on the training field, no doubt pondering the idea in his head. "I will allow you to train—" His sentence was cut off by Eva jumping off the ground with a squeal and giving him a kiss on his cheek. "I will allow you to train," he started again, "using the simulators only. Not with any of my guards."

Abruptly, she stopped jumping up and down. "What? Why can't I train with the guards?"

"Yeah, why can't Eva train with the guards?" Lo'Ren asked. Taio peered her way. "I get it, you're not talking to me."

"Eva, they are royal guards, warriors. Look at them. They will think I am belittling them if I send you in there with them. Be glad that I am allowing you to use the training simulators."

She started to balk, but stopped short, snapping her mouth closed. He was right. Being able to do some kind of training was better than sitting in the grass, plotting a way to get closer to the training field.

"Okay, but you still have to get me one of those *jango* things."

\* \* \* \* \*

Early the next day, under the protective canopy Taio had erected for her, she stood in front of a training simulator with sweat pouring off her body. When Taio restricted her to using the training simulators, he failed to mention they were replicas of the enemies that were common to the Drazlan and Sonis people.

So to say the least, she was more than a little taken aback when Rasha led her to an equipment room that held seven life-like alien simulators to choose from. Hell, she didn't need the guards. She could have her fun with these for years to come.

She picked out the ugliest-looking one of the bunch. It looked the same as the Loconuist and she planned to kick some Earth-invading, human-enslaving alien ass.

With Rasha's help, she was able to set it to the training level she desired. At first, she started off slow, warming up to full fighting mode. But after noticing the guards watching her, she decided to kick it up a notch.

Taio said the guards would not train with a female and would feel it was beneath them. Ha! She laughed to herself. She was making mincemeat of this robot and loving it.

Lo'Ren sat at the edge of the field, watching her, positioning herself at a good vantage point. The girl was no Ally, but she wasn't bad either. Taio had removed her from the cleaning crew and had given her the official job of "friend to Eva".

Yesterday, Eva tried, unsuccessfully, to shake her after lunch. Wherever she hid, Lo'Ren popped up. That girl was taking her job very seriously. This morning Eva decided to take a different approach. She was Batman and Lo'Ren was her sidekick, Robin.

Aside from Lo'Ren, Rasha and Jor'Dan came by and watched. But she was really trying to impress the rest of the guards, who were watching her out of the corners of their eyes.

"You have much talent, Eva," Rasha said.

"Wow, you approve? Thank you, Rasha. It means a lot coming from you."

"The guards seem well impressed with your moves and skill. We don't practice hand-to-hand combat anymore, but it seems to be a skill that we may need again. Are all Earthlings trained in this type of combat as you are?" Rasha asked.

"We are called humans, and yes, most of us are trained as youngsters in martial arts. It is an Earth tradition." Well, it wasn't an outright lie. She did say "most". So when Rasha and Jor'Dan exchanged a look between themselves, she didn't feel all that guilty.

By midday, she was semi-surrounded by four guards. Rasha had gone to Taio and gotten permission to have some of the guards, those who were interested, watch her train with the simulator. Although she was still pummeling the simulator for now, she was sure that soon she would be accepted to train with the guards.

All seemed to be going well, except for a small group of guards who were laughing and pointing her way. Knowing they mocked her, she ignored them. This was not the first time she had been laughed at. If these guards wanted to upset her with their taunts, they really had a lot to learn. They needed to hang out with elementary school kids.

"Do not mind them, Eva," Rasha said.

"Don't worry about me. I'm having the most fun I've had in years!" She somersaulted over the simulator, landing at its back and giving it one hell of a kidney punch, well, assuming its kidney would be in that spot.

"When you are all ready to see real warriors train, make your way to us!" one of the guards yelled.

She looked over to see the guard from the group of hecklers motioning his way.

"And after you see how a guard fights, come back and watch a girl." For emphasis, she dropped to the ground and swiped her foot underneath the simulator, knocking it flat on the ground.

"Ouch." Jor'Dan smiled.

Jumping up, she halfheartedly gave a bow to the guards standing around her, who had begun to clap.

"You think you know how to fight, but you are nothing here." The same guard sneered, now walking her way, fists balled up at his sides.

His face was red and full of rage and his lips were pressed in a hard line. Rasha stepped in front of Eva, blocking his pursuit.

"Coyl, don't come any farther. She has permission from Taio to be on the training field," Rasha said through gritted teeth.

"His judgment is obviously clouded by the slickness of her pussy, since it is well known that he fucks the bitch night and day," Coyl said.

"Get out of my sight before I hold you down and let her beat you myself," Rasha said.

Eva stepped from behind Rasha. "Thank you for the offer, Rasha, but I wouldn't need you to hold him down for me. Anyone can see he's past his prime and hoping, wishing and...no, praying that I'll knock him down. Because it's as close as he'll ever get to having a woman touch him."

Coyl let out a war cry and ran toward her. Rasha dropped in a low stance, about to take the brute head on, preventing him from reaching Eva. Although she appreciated the gesture, she had a different idea. She had never been known to let others fight for her. Without a moment's hesitation, she took off running toward Rasha and Coyl. Using Rasha's leg and shoulder as steps, she leaped over him and extended her leg, aiming it right at Coyl's face.

"Humph," was the only sound that came out of Coyl's mouth before he fell backward in an unconscious heap.

Keeping her stance low, she circled slowly. These guards were trained to watch each other's backs. She was prepared to take on anyone else who came her way.

Instead of a fight, she was met with applause from the guards before they returned to what they had been doing.

Slowly rising, she watched as Rasha walked toward her.

"I think you may have some requests from the other guards to help with their training," Rasha said after stopping in front of her.

"You think so? They won't be upset that I took down one of their own?" She looked over to Coyl's body. Jor'Dan was now standing over his unconscious body, nudging him with a boot.

"That's exactly why they would want some training tips. The hard part will be getting Taio to agree to it."

As if on cue, Taio came stalking into view. The guards made certain to keep out of the way as their large king walked toward them. Guards who were training near her inconspicuously moved farther away.

"Rasha! Ship told me there was a disturbance on the training field. What's going on here?"

"Nothing that should have caused Ship to be alarmed," Rasha replied.

"No?"

"No." Rasha wasn't lying. In fact, she had taken care of the situation effectively.

"Lo'Ren?"

Lo'Ren shrugged when Taio turned her way. Her mouth was sealed shut. Eva loved her immediately.

She silently prayed no one would give them away. If Taio found out Coyl had almost jumped on her, she could kiss training on the field goodbye. It wouldn't even matter that most of his guards didn't mind her presence here. One idiot would ruin her chances of returning.

Taio looked around, taking in the surroundings. His eyes settled on Coyl. "Great Ancients! Is he dead?"

Eva and Rasha looked over at the heap lying on the ground. Just as Coyl started to groan, Jor'Dan gave him another hard kick in the face.

"He was injured while training," Jor'Dan said.

# Chapter Thirteen

**ᔕ**

"You are still going through with it?" Rasha asked Taio.

They were both watching the dinner entertainment. Three females swayed their hips in shimmering see-through material to music as they danced in the center of the dining area.

"Yes, I am still going through with it. Nothing has changed for me." Taio glanced at Eva, who was sitting next to Lo'Ren, smiling as she watched the provocative dance. As he watched the pair, he decided he had made the right decision when he brought the two together. Unsure at first if the quirky female would be good company for Eva, now he was quite satisfied.

"Have you told Eva?"

"I will. But it will not make a difference. My plans have not changed."

"I thought you were getting closer to her. You two seem to be a good match."

Taio blew out a breath. "She has almost everything that I hoped to find in a suitable mate. She is beautiful, smart and brave, she has nice-sized breasts and the roundest ass I've ever seen."

"Whoa. Enough, my friend. I know how much you enjoy your human. I believe everyone who happens to be in earshot of your coupling knows how much you enjoy her."

"As much as I enjoy her, I cannot create a match with her."

"Why not?"

"She will not bring what we need to Sonis. I need to create a match with someone who can bring more business to the people of Sonis. If I take her as my mate, we will remain in the same position that we are in now."

"I think we have done quite well for ourselves. We receive families who migrate from the home world every day."

Taio pondered the thought. He would want nothing more than to be bonded with Eva. But she could not offer him or his people what they needed. It would be selfish for him to only consider his needs and not look at the bigger picture. Yes, families came in droves from Drazlan to Sonis, but without a means to provide for themselves, his people would be forever dependent on him.

His only option would be to find a mate in name only, all the while keeping Eva for himself. Eva would agree because he was all she had. He was sure it was still an acceptable plan for the both of them.

"What do you plan to do with Eva once you find a mate? Let her live on the palace grounds? Once you give up your claim on her, I expect the guards will be falling over themselves to claim her. Are you prepared for her to find a mate as well?"

Taio stilled. *Never. I would kill any male who tried to touch her.*

"She would have no need for a mate. I will still have her. It is practiced in many cultures throughout the galaxy. Who's to say it was not practiced on her home world as well? She would have to move from my personal quarters, of course. But I have no problem with setting her up in one of the apartments on the other side of the palace."

Taio tried to control his temper. He cared for Rasha just as he did his own brother, but if he kept up this talk of Eva finding a mate, he would gut him.

"Oh and you think Eva will abide by this new arrangement?" Rasha jerked his head in Eva's direction.

"Of course she will. Why wouldn't she?" He seemed to be trying to convince himself more than his friend.

"It may be widely practiced in this galaxy, but what if it is not in her culture? Have you even talked to her about it?"

"No, I haven't. But it will not matter. She will stay with me. She has nowhere else to go. Eva will understand that it is for the best."

He blew out a breath. "I am responsible for everyone who you see around you. This is extremely important to us. We need to make a good alliance to bring prosperity to our world." Taio could feel himself growing more agitated by the minute. This conversation was pointless and he didn't want to talk about it.

"I thought we were already prosperous," Rasha replied. "We have Sonis Mercenary and Sonis Gold. We are one of the richest worlds in this galaxy. What more do we need?"

Taio's fist slammed down on the table. "What we need is more businesses to ensure our world will thrive. We need visitors to flock to our markets to buy the local goods."

Exasperated, he ran a hand across his hair. "We can accomplish this quicker and easier if I am able to form a successful bond. The right mate will help bring more visitors, settlers and businesses to Sonis. Sonis will need to survive on its own without the help of my businesses. I want the people of Sonis to be independent."

"Taio, you are not your father. You never were, nor will be."

It wasn't easy growing up in the royal Xochis household. He had tried time and time again to forget his childhood. His father had made the people of Drazlan, including himself, subject to his every whim. His father owned the largest company on Drazlan and "employed" the people of Drazlan to work for him.

"How do you intend to find a mate?" Rasha asked as Taio sat in silence.

Taio let his friend's question pull him out of his trance. "I was thinking of a party."

"A party?"

"Yes, a party. I am thinking of inviting eligible females here for a party," Taio said, satisfied with the decision.

"Well, good luck with that. Be prepared for every female species in the surrounding galaxies to come running here in hopes of mating with one of the richest males."

"I'm not opening my doors to just anyone." Taio shook his head. "I want to extend invitations only to those who I know can help bring prosperity to Sonis."

"Which females do you have in mind?"

"I have a few in mind. But I need help finding enough to choose from."

Rasha raised his eyebrow.

"I'm going to ask my mother for help."

"This ought to be really good." Rasha choked out a laugh.

His mother was known for her wildly extravagant parties. Any good news, or the possibility of good news, was a reason to throw a party.

Taio's eyes wandered again to where Eva sat. He was having a hard time keeping his eyes off her. The thought of bonding with someone else was not sitting right with him and he would never release her to another male.

As if she could feel him watching her, Eva turned around and met his eyes. He wanted her, here and now. His cock throbbed and hardened between his thighs. Eva playfully licked her lips. She was ready for him. She was always ready.

His cock twitched in response. Without a word to his friend, he rose, walked through the dancers, sending them scattering out of his path, picked Eva off the pillows and slung her over his shoulder.

"Remind me to tell you about cavemen sometime." She giggled.

\* \* \* \* \*

Screams. She covered her ears but couldn't keep the screams from filtering through. Her eyes scanned the panicked crowd. Everyone scattered and cowered, hiding in the smallest of places while the Loconuist stomped their way through the makeshift tent city.

If the Loconuist were in the belly of the spacecraft, it meant one thing, trouble. Her heart picked up speed. It was another "taking". The monstrous lizards stopped only to grab humans, picking them out indiscriminately. Men, women and children, it didn't matter.

Her eyes darted through the frenzy. Where was Allysan? "Ally!" she yelled. Eva pushed through the crowd. "Ally!"

The Loconuist were coming her way. She dropped to a low crouch as everyone else panicked and pushed around her. Through the sea of legs, she spotted a wide-eyed Ally staring back at her.

Eva held Ally's stare, willing her to be quiet and patient. They needed to stay unnoticed. Fear was written all across her friend's face. Ally flicked her eyes upward before her crazed eyes came back to Eva's. Ally opened her mouth to scream.

Eva shook her head. "No," she mouthed.

Time stood still. The air grew thick and hot. She forced air through her lungs and out. A hot drop of liquid landed on her forehead and rolled steadily down to her eyebrow.

She lifted her hand to catch the drop before it hit her eye. Scooping the glob away, she brought her hand to eye level. Slime coated her fingers.

No. Her eyes filled with tears. It was time. She didn't need to look up to see what stood over her, waiting.

Searing pain tore through her shoulder as large claws dug through the skin and gripped the bone. No! No! No!

\* \* \* \* \*

"Eva!" She opened her eyes. Taio's face was inches from hers. "Wake up, little one. You are having a nightmare."

She pushed herself up to a sitting position. Wetness dripped from her forehead. She wiped it away and looked at her hand. Sweat, not slime.

"I'm okay." She scanned the room, taking in her surroundings. She wasn't on the Loconuist spacecraft. The Loconuist weren't here. She was safe. But Ally...

She covered her hands with her face. She'd lost Ally. Taio pulled her closer to him.

"What were you dreaming about?"

"Them." She didn't want to say their name anymore.

"You are safe here."

"I am, but Ally...I lost her." The tears rolled easily down her cheek. She punched at the pillow. "Damn it! I need to find her. I have to find her. She's out there all alone."

"Come here." Taio lay back down, pulling her on top of him. "Go back to sleep. If anyone can find her, it is Ship. But I can assure you he won't find her tonight."

She nuzzled into his arms. Her protests died away as sleep claimed her once again.

Late the next morning, Eva rolled over to find Taio's side of the bed empty. Taio had since gotten up and was no doubt in his office tending to "official Sonis business". That man worked too damn hard. Taking care of Sonis was definitely more than a full-time job.

Ship explained to her that Sonis had a total population of fifty thousand people, which definitely wasn't enough to occupy an entire moon. He was working hard, trying to make Sonis a thriving world, and she was proud of him for that. He ruled over the people on Sonis, but he had their utmost safety, livelihood and happiness in mind with every decision he made.

Before taking a quick dip in the large pool that passed for a bathtub, she straightened their room, made the bed and folded the clothes that he'd left scattered around the floor. She was aware that as soon as she left, there would be someone in to clean up, but she felt compelled to do it herself. There were no maids in the orphanage and definitely not in her small apartment back in Michigan.

She donned her training jumpsuit. The special material let the wearer's skin breathe while providing protection from the penetration of sharp objects. With her new *jango* strapped to her back and Lo'Ren by her side, she left for the training field.

She had to give it to Taio, ever since Lo'Ren started shadowing her, the other females in the palace were being nicer. Even now, as she walked through the halls, the females she passed nodded to her. Eva hesitantly returned their greetings. These same females had previously turned their noses up at her. What a difference a week made, she thought.

She didn't know what the big deal was. So what if she liked to be able to take care of herself? Apparently, that belief made the local female population avoid her as if she carried the plague. Plus, if they could accept Lo'Ren, they should accept her. Lo'Ren was pink with hot-pink hair, for God's sake!

"When is Taio going to give up this idea that his whore can train on the same field as warriors?" Coyl said as Eva led her training simulator out to the field.

Ignoring him as she had for the past couple of days was getting harder by the day.

"Whores are good for one thing only." Coyl laughed, holding his hand between his legs.

As the days progressed, his audience had significantly dwindled from a handful to two. Briefly, she had thought to tell Taio but had decided against it. If Taio found out there was trouble on the field and it was because of her, he might take her training privileges away. If she had to suck it up and deal with this asshole, she would, in order to keep her training time.

She turned her favorite training simulator on and started through the warm-up exercise. Without warning, the simulator immediately jumped from the warm-up stage to stage four, the most advanced stage. She was in a world of trouble.

The large tail whipped around, knocking her down. She fell to the ground. The sand and dirt temporarily blinded her as it mushroomed around her. As it cleared, her vision was of a large, scaly foot that tried to smash her head in. She rolled out of the way. The simulator had definitely been tampered with.

"Help!" She leaped to her feet as she avoided the green foot that landed inches from her face.

As she struggled, Coyl and his friends laughed and smacked each other on their backs. Her only hope was to try to overtake the simulator. With every move she completed, she tried to turn the stupid thing off. Appearing out of nowhere, Rasha lunged at the simulator's back and disengaged it. The simulator froze with its claws reaching out to grab her. She wanted to throw up.

"Eva, why would you set it for the most advanced setting? It could have killed you."

She leaned over and put both of her hands on her knees, trying to catch her breath.

"You think? I set it to the warm-up stage. It jumped to level four without me programming it," she said between hard breaths. She began coughing, her body trying to clear the dirt, dust and sand from her lungs.

"It cannot jump to level four without being preset for it." Rasha tinkered with the simulator's control console.

"I didn't set it to kill me." Her voice dripped with sarcasm.

Straightening, she brushed the sand and dirt from her clothes. Aside from a few scratches and small cuts, there wasn't any major damage done. Nothing that couldn't be explained away as regular training injuries. Taio would not hear about this if she could help it.

Coyl and his friends moved farther off, still laughing and smiling, clearly finding the humor in her near-death experience.

Rasha followed Eva's eyes to the laughing men and started toward them.

"Rasha, please don't go over there." She ran to his side, pulling at his arm. "If you do, it'll only cause more trouble for me on the training field."

She trotted next to him as he continued his pursuit. "More trouble than trying to kill you?" he asked.

He was right. She wanted to train and not get killed in the process. She nodded her head in response and stopped. Rasha made his way over to Coyl in five long strides.

"You will go to your room and stay there. You will await my direction," Rasha said. Coyl turned in her direction and growled. Rasha pulled his *jango* from its sheath and pointed it at him. "If you come near her again, I will kill you."

"You aren't going to make me leave the palace for that whore!"

"Leave the field, Coyl, and take your accomplices with you."

"I was just playing a joke!"

"A joke? She could have been killed!"

"That's why the training field isn't meant for females or whores." Coyl spit on the ground. "Taio should learn to keep his whores in his bed. His father always knew the place of whores." With that, Rasha smacked the guard with the broad side of the weapon, sending him flying.

She turned and walked away, feeling embarrassed and humiliated. Taio was sure to forbid her from the training field now.

# Chapter Fourteen

ജ

Eva stood at the kitchen door, feeling defeated and depressed. She had surely lost her only outlet on this rock. If she were home, she would have opened up the fridge and let loose.

But she wasn't home, and instead of her refrigerator door, her feet led her to the next best place, the palace kitchen. She could have gone back to the royal quarters with Lo'Ren and pigged out, but if Taio was there, she would be forced to explain what happened. Right now, she wasn't in the mood.

"Eva, what are you doing here?" Eva blinked in surprise as a round woman who towered over her turned her way. "Why aren't you on the training field?"

Hours later and with a belly full of a substance close to ice cream, she officially felt better. The cooks had been more than welcoming to her. Now all she had to do was go back to the training field, although it was the last place she wanted to be. But of all the stupid things she could have done, she had forgotten her *jango* there. Taio had it specially made for her, she wasn't going to be humiliated and lose her *jango* all in the same day.

*Maybe I can ask Ship to have Lo'Ren pick it up for me?* Lo'Ren had left with a stomachache a little while ago. The chilled milk substance hadn't set well in her new friend's belly.

Turning the corner, she stopped short of colliding with the last person she had ever wanted to see again, Coyl.

Her eyes immediately surveyed her surroundings. Coyl had two other guards flanking his sides. The four of them were the only people in the hallway. His eyes were bloodshot red and focused on her.

*Shit, trouble. Where the hell is Taio?*

"Excuse me." She tried to bypass him and the other guards.

When she stepped to the side, Coyl stepped, blocking her. She pursed her lips and stepped left; he growled low in his throat and again matched her step.

"Let me pass. I don't want any more trouble than you've already caused." She tried again to step around him. He blocked her path and chuckled.

"You are not going anywhere, whore," Coyl snarled.

Her gut churned. She knew instantly Coyl had come looking for a fight. She could handle one, maybe two, but three royal guards? She'd seen them train, royal guards were some of the best warriors she had ever seen. She straightened her back. All she had to do was hold them off until Taio came.

"Call me what you want, but we both know who has the pussy. I don't need to bring reinforcements to fight you."

Coyl laughed again. "I didn't bring them to help me fight. I brought them so we could take turns breaking you." He grabbed and fondled his cock. The other two laughed in unison, slapping each other's backs. "We are going to use you up, whore."

Eva tsked and turned to the other men. "If he promised you that this would be easy, he lied." She put one hand on her hip and the other on her chin. "And maybe when I'm done breaking all of you, I'll give you over to the rest of the guards for a good fucking."

All three snapped their eyes back to her, one letting out a feral growl. She loosened her stance, expecting it to get worse before it got better.

One of the males looked over at Coyl warily. That was all she needed to determine he was the weak link of the group.

Light on her feet and without making a sound, she sidestepped and planted a fierce kick to his knee. *Crack.* The guard's howl erupted throughout the air.

The kick shattered his kneecap. Her face scrunched in anger, knowing that all it would take was a few hours in the healing tank to completely heal him. *Bummer.* At least this fool would be in excruciating pain until he got there.

That thought gave her pause to smile.

"Crazy bitch," Coyl snarled. His friend lay writhing in pain on the ground.

"Just in case you need help keeping score, I have one and you have zero," she said.

Coyl rushed forward with a war cry.

She stepped to the side as he ran past her, planting a hard elbow on his back, hitting him in the kidney.

"Humph," he said.

The next guard swung at her head. Ducking under his blow, she grabbed his testicles firmly in her hand, gripping harder against his struggles. Obviously she didn't have a firm enough hold on him if he still thought to move on his own, she thought.

She used his testicles to steer him around, keeping him planted firmly between her and Coyl. Every time Coyl tried to come around, she moved the guard to block his way. Using the guard as a barrier, Eva reached around with her free hand and punched Coyl, knowing each punch that connected would do enough damage to eventually slow the crazed guard down.

She punched and punched, using the unfortunate guard as a shield, until finally the brute begin to sway. The pain in his testicles too much for him to bear any longer, he dropped to his knees and slumped over.

Coyl looked at the man on the floor, then back to Eva.

"Two to zero." She plastered a smile back on her face.

Coyl flared his nostrils, clenched his fists and slowly advanced forward. Eva kicked at him, trying to land another blow to the knee. What worked for one might work for the other.

No such luck. Coyl caught her foot.

"Did you think it was going to be that easy?" he said mockingly.

"Yes."

Using his hand to stabilize her foot, she swung her body around, grabbing his shoulders and propelling herself up to his neck, sandwiching it between her thighs. Startled, he let her go and reached up to grab her legs. Tightening her hold, she used her knees as a vise around his neck.

Taking his head in both her hands, she dug her fingers in his hair. With one fluid movement, she jerked his head to the right.

Coyl went still and dropped slowly to the floor.

She made the slow descent with him. Only after her feet touched the ground, with Coyl's head hitting right after, did she look up to see Taio, Rasha and Jor'Dan standing in front of her.

Taio surveyed the scene before him. One of his men lay in a crying heap, holding his knee. The man obviously needed medical attention, but he could wait a little while longer.

The other man was unconscious, his hands between his legs and knees drawn up in a fetal position.

Coyl was no doubt dead. Taio had watched the light leave the guard's eyes as Eva snapped his neck.

Then there was Eva. She stood with her legs spread apart, arms at her sides. Her head was down slightly, her hair in a disheveled mess around her face and her eyes watching him.

It was the same look she had when he found her on Xenaris. Her mind still in battle mode, not yet fully back from where it had gone. Locking his eyes with hers, he walked forward slowly. Her breath increasing with each step he took.

Reaching her, he picked her up and held her in his arms. Prepared for her to fight against him, he held her tight. Her body tensed briefly, and then with a slight shudder, she began to shake violently in his arms.

"Clean up this mess and get them to the infirmary." He walked away with Eva safe in his arms. "Slowly."

Without a word, he walked through the palace halls. He didn't expect her to talk to him and he didn't try to make her. Instead, she kept her head buried in his chest and her body trembled.

After Rasha told him what happened, Taio had gone to Coyl's room to ban him and those who helped him from the palace. Only after reaching an empty room did Ship put out an alert. He, Rasha and JorDan had run through the palace to save her. The entire time, he thought his heart would explode. The thought of not reaching her in time had him in a panic.

Holding her tighter, he brought her closer to his body. He spent the entire trip cradling Eva in his arms, thinking about how vulnerable she actually was. He was responsible for her and had almost lost her.

Everyone in his path moved out of the way. They didn't need to know what transpired, but they knew something was wrong. Their king had murder in his eyes. He reached his private quarters and paused only momentarily as the scanner made its verification. Mazel met him at the door, but he shooed her away before continuing to his bedroom.

Once there, he gently laid her on the bed. She put her head in her hands, hiding her face from him. He tugged gently at them, trying to move them out of his way, but she held them firmly in place. Soft sobs came from behind them. Leaning down, he placed a light kiss on her shoulder.

Then another.

And another.

He trailed kisses all down her arm. Lingering at her elbow, he gave it a little nip, working his way to her hand. He trailed kisses from her wrist to the tip of her fingers. There, he slowly let his mouth cover two of her fingers and pulled them between his lips, running his tongue across the tips. He slid his tongue between two fingers and flickered where they joined, feeling her fingers go slack in his mouth.

From behind a hand, she moaned, until finally her hands slid away from her face, revealing dark lashes that were wet with tears.

He abandoned her fingers and leaned over her. "You are so beautiful, little one."

He placed light kisses around her eyes and followed the tear tracks down her face to her swollen lips. Releasing a groan, he pulled her swollen bottom lip into his mouth, sucking and pulling. "You are so very strong."

"I was so scared." Eva reached up and cradled his head with her hands. "I thought they were going to kill me."

"I am sorry that I was not there to protect you." He stroked the side of her cheek. "Why did you keep this from me, little one? I would have banished Coyl from Sonis the first time he started trouble."

"I'm sorry. I should have told you. But I was afraid you would stop me from training."

He cocked his head to the side. "I might have." When she started to object, he cut her off. "That was before. You have proved to be one of the finest fighters on Sonis."

"You really think so?" she whispered.

"One of the best. But you are still mine to protect. I won't let anyone hurt you."

"Promise?"

"Yes."

He crushed his mouth over hers, parting her lips with his tongue, his meeting hers. She pulled him closer to her. Her tongue tangled with his. Taio slid his hand under her shirt, finding her breast.

Eva moaned as he touched and caressed her, slowly massaging, enjoying the feeling of her soft skin against his large, calloused hand. When he took the pad of his rough thumb and teased her erect, plump nipple, Eva moaned under his touch and arched her back.

"Let go. I will protect you. You will never be alone again," he whispered.

He latched on to her other nipple, pulling and sucking, as she buried both hands in his hair. Taking his hand, she guided it to the spot he loved to rub most. Her clit. There, he slowly rubbed the hard nub. Moaning, she spread her legs wider before finally wrapping her ankles around his back.

He used his fingers to massage her nub and then dipped them deep into her weeping sheath. Her walls gripped his finger as he slid in and out. She bucked beneath him, bringing her hips up to meet his finger, begging for more. He sucked and teased her nipples, enjoying how she reacted to him.

Only for him.

He slid another finger inside to join the other. She instantly threw her head back and gasped, her walls contracting around them. Gliding them in and out a few more strokes before he finally had enough, he couldn't wait any longer.

She let out a small whimper of protest as he removed them.

"Please…more."

Instead of giving her what she begged for, he moved onto his knees. He grabbed the top of her pants, pulled them down and flung them across the room. He discarded his own shirt and pants even faster. His cock bounced and twitched, anticipating the snugness and warmth that awaited him.

Eva's eyes glazed over as she stared at him. His muscles flexed as his body readied for her, moving in for the kill. Positioning himself between her legs, he held her by the knees and urged them to open even farther to accommodate his size. His cock grew even harder as he watched her dripping wet pussy.

Leaning forward, he pressed the head against her tight, slick opening. He leaned in more, pressing the head farther inside. He inhaled sharply as the head finally breached the tight entryway of bliss. He pulled out just a little and pressed forward again, going a little deeper than before.

She whimpered as he continued his merciless descent until he was halfway in. Only then did he stop, close his eyes and let them roll back in his head. He could travel the universe and never find a pussy as good as hers.

After a few moments, she twirled her hips in circular motions before bringing them up to take more.

"No, little one." He put a hand on her hip, stopping her from rising any farther. "I won't be able to contain myself if you keep doing that. I don't want to hurt you."

"I don't want you to hold back. I can take it," she whispered. Eva moved his hand and brought her hips up in one swift motion, taking more of him.

He groaned and she moaned, her slickness overwhelming him.

With a loud cry, he reached under her, gripping her ass roughly in both hands, lifting her hips higher. She wrapped her arms around his neck and her legs squeezed tighter around his back. Holding onto her tightly, he pumped into her deep and hard. The faster he moved, the louder she screamed. Her fingernails dug into his back, legs pulling him in deeper.

She wanted it all.

She could take all he gave her.

She was his little warrior.

She clawed and screamed as her pussy convulsed and erupted, covering his cock with her slick juices. After two more thrusts, he joined her, spurting his cum deep inside her. Her pussy milked him for every drop.

Lying with half of his body on her and the other on the bed, he kept her legs around his waist. He wanted her close at hand when his cock got hard again. She stroked his hair slowly, his breathing started to slow and he drifted off to sleep.

# Chapter Fifteen

ഗ

"My sweet baby, how are you doing?" Taio closed his eyes and inwardly cringed at the familiar high-pitched voice.

His mother had arrived.

He turned to greet her. "Hello, Mother. I trust your trip was satisfactory?"

He opened his arms as his mother came to him, returning his hug and planting a soft kiss on each cheek. Although it was a standard greeting for loved ones, his face reddened at the public display of motherly affection. Rasha making light kissing noises beside him didn't help matters either.

"The trip was as well as could be expected." His mother shot a quick look in his father's direction.

His mother and father had an arranged marriage and it was well known they did not get along. They tried to avoid each other at all costs, only being in the same room for diplomatic purposes. He guessed that helping him find a mate was considered a diplomatic purpose.

"Greetings, King Xochis," Taio said. He addressed his father by his official title, as he preferred.

"Greetings, Prince Taio." His father nodded slightly, choosing to call him a prince, even though he was King of Sonis. "I hear you have acquired a new species. Let me take a look at her."

Taio stilled. While he could let his father's slight of word go, he could not tolerate his father's interest in Eva. Taio hadn't told his father about Eva and didn't plan on it. Someone was feeding, or had fed, information to him. Bedding as many females as possible was among the many high qualities his father had. Taio made a mental note to keep a guard with Eva at all times with strict instructions she should never be left alone with his father.

"I am afraid she is not for public use," he said without a hint of remorse. "But there are many other species coming within the next day or so for the festivities."

His mother became very still under his arm. He didn't like to talk about his father's transgressions in front of her, even if she was well aware of her mate's extramarital affairs.

"Prince Taio!" A smile crossed his lips as his sister came into view across the room. Saia had on a red gown, accentuating her golden skin tone. Her red-colored slippers made a soft padding noise on the floor as she ran his way.

At seventeen birth cycles, Saia was the highlight of his life. Shortly after she had her fifteenth birth cycle, he'd petitioned his father to send Saia to live with him, wanting to offer his little sister a better life. He knew it was only a matter of time before his father bonded her in a contract for monetary or political gain and that would be the day he would have to kill the king.

Reaching him, she ran right into his arms and, despite his size, almost knocked him and his mother down.

"Ship told me you bought me something while you were on Xenaris!" Saia said.

"Really, Saia, princesses do not behave in such a manner!" his mother said, exasperated. Taio smiled, this was not the first time his mother had talked to Saia about her behavior. As if on cue, his father turned and walked off.

"I am sorry, Mother, I couldn't help myself," Saia said. She wrapped her arms tighter around his midsection.

He released his mother and returned his sister's embrace, lifting the younger female off the ground, kissing both cheeks. Saia giggled in return. "You get prettier each time I lay eyes on you."

Saia was two heads shorter than he was, with the same lavender-colored eyes that he and his siblings had inherited from their mother. Her thick black hair hung down in cascading waves below her waist.

"Paw. You always say that." She playfully hit his arm. "Ship promised I would like my gift. Let me see it."

"I have your gift right here." He patted his jacket pocket. "But it seems you lost what little manners I remember you having."

"Oh! Don't play games with me, Taio. Please. I promise to be on my best behavior." She jumped from one foot to the other, waiting for him to retrieve the necklace from his pocket.

Bringing the necklace out, he fastened it around her neck.

"Oh it's beautiful! Mother, isn't it lovely?" She turned to show the necklace to their mother. "It matches my eyes. Thank you so much, Taio," Saia said before her mother had a chance to answer. She wrapped her arms around his neck, hugging him tight.


Eva stood in the elaborately furnished ballroom, watching the exchange between Taio and his family from afar. It was obvious from the way his face lit up that he cared for his mother and sister deeply. Even without an introduction, she would have been able to spot them.

Another male walked into the room, greeting Taio, Saia and his mother with a hug. The new visitor had to be his younger brother, Kiehle. He was almost a replica of Taio. Biting her fingernails, a habit she had thought she lost a long time ago, she looked on. Was he going to call her over, she wondered, secretly hoping he would.

As she watched them, her chest began to constrict, the old feelings of abandonment and loneliness started to surround her. She brought her hand up to her heart. She imagined the loneliness taking root inside as if it were a weed, winding its way around her heart and smothering it. Would there ever be a time when she had family to greet her? On this new world, she was no more than an orphan. Now she was one who had also lost a planet.

She slowly rubbed her hand over her chest, trying to ease some of the tension away. No such luck. She could feel her eyes begin to water. Blinking back tears, she turned away from the reunion. She would not embarrass herself by crying in public.

*Crap, what is coming over me? Why am I so fucking emotional?*

Eva hadn't been sure if she should even attend the welcome ball for the royal family. Only after Lo'Ren and Mazel had made such a fuss about it did she finally agree to come. Although Taio had not broached the subject of her attending at all, he didn't seem to mind when he found out.

She looked down at the blue silk gown with matching slippers. Mazel had picked out the ensemble. Lo'Ren even weighed in and approved her choice. Thanks to Mazel, her hair was up in an intricate design, held in place by diamond pins.

Eva reached for her hair, mentally counting each exquisite pin. *Eleven.* The thought of walking around with the expensive hair decorations made her nervous.

She didn't claim to be the prettiest girl in the room, but she was happy about how it all had turned out. If she was to meet the royal family, she would at least look presentable. She tried to remember the last time she even wore a dress.

*This is a bit over my head.* She scanned the room, fighting the urge to leave.

The only reason she stayed rooted in place was because of Mazel's efforts. Well, that, and she had also promised Lo'Ren she would tell her all about it tomorrow. If she left now, her new friend would bug her for days about the injustice of not being able to attend and not getting the scoop about the party.

"You must be Eva." A female's voice intruded on her thoughts.

Eva jumped at the sound of her name. Damn, she was losing her touch. A couple of months ago, no one would have been able to sneak up on her. She turned around, surprised to see Taio's mother talking to her. *Shit.* Neither Taio nor Mazel had explained what the protocol was for greeting royalty.

"Umm...hello, yes, I'm Eva." She stuck out her hand, but quickly brought it in when his mother stared at it, confused.

She then attempted a curtsy, the kind she had seen on multiple television shows. His mother lowered her eyes and looked to be searching the ground for something. *Wrong again.* Eva straightened; this was not going as she had hoped. "Nice to meet you," she finally said.

"Nice to meet you too." The queen gave her head a slight nod. "I hear you are sharing a bed with my son."

Eva's breath caught in her throat. *Damn, this lady sure is straightforward.*

"Will you continue to stay in my son's room while the guests are here?" the queen asked.

"What...?"

*Maybe they were really conservative people.* That would explain why his mother disapproved of her staying in Taio's room. "I could leave if you think it would be best?"

This was her first time meeting his mother, or anyone's mother, for that matter, and she was not going to ruin it by doing or saying anything to upset her.

"That would be best." His mother smiled warmly in return. "I am afraid that if you remained in his bed, he might become...distracted."

"Distracted?"

"Well, yes. I am not a male, but I should think it would be extremely difficult to find a future mate with a concubine in my bed. That would be difficult, even for a male."

"Picking out a future mate?" Now she was really confused. What was going on here? At no time had he mentioned anything about finding a "future mate". *I will kill him.*

"Taio did not explain this to you?"

"No, I'm afraid that he didn't. I'm sorry to intrude on his party. I really am." She tried to force the words out of her mouth.

"Tsk. I thought he would have explained his plans to you before now." The queen shook her head. "It doesn't matter. What will be, will be."

"He never told me. Are you sure?" she asked. Was his mother mistaken? *A mate?* She didn't expect marriage from him, but she thought there had been some kind of connection between the two of them.

"Well, of course I am sure. He invited me here to help pick out a potential candidate."

"Oh." Her eyes scanned the room, finally taking it all in. Every female in attendance positioned themselves in Taio's line of sight and watched him. *Potential candidates.*

They all knew the nature of this gathering. Everyone here must know. *Everyone except for me.*

"I can see why he is enthralled with you." His mother's eyes scanned her from head to toe. "Unfortunately, I think he intends to keep you."

"Do you mean make me his mate?"

The queen laughed. "No, no. Not as a mate. You would never do. He is a king and you are but a mere...slave."

*A mere slave.*

*Ouch.*

"Oh I understand," Eva said. "I think I should remove my things from his room then." Turning away from his mother, she looked back over her shoulder. The queen was already making her way back across the room to her family.

She picked up her pace. She had one goal and one goal only — reach the exit before the tears completely overtook her eyes.

"Where are you going?" Mazel reached out and grabbed for her arm. She had not even noticed his assistant, who had hurried to her side.

She turned red-rimmed eyes to Mazel. Hissing, she slapped her outstretched hand away. "Why didn't you tell me?"

Mazel's mouth opened to a perfect O as she stepped back, bringing her hand to her chest. "I am sorry, Eva. I thought..."

Eva turned away and ran out of the room, pushing past anyone who stood in her way, not hearing the rest of Mazel's words. What did it matter anyway?

*How could he have done this to me?* The same thought repeated in her head as she ran through the palace. Did everyone know the "gathering" was planned so he could find a mate? She'd stood there, hoping he would call her over and introduce her to his family.

*Ha! A mere slave.* She mentally beat herself up for even thinking she could have been a part of that love. All the while he was planning to discard her for another, as if she were trash.

She ran toward their shared rooms, tears of betrayal pouring down her cheeks.

She ripped off the foolish dress, kicked off the useless shoes and took the ridiculous pins out of her hair. She grabbed and threw on the only thing comfortable to her, her fighting suit and boots.

She was gathering her belongings, as meager as they were, when Taio arrived. "Eva, little one, what are you doing?"

"What the hell do you think I'm doing?" she said through clenched teeth. How dare he put her through this humiliation and then waltz in here as if nothing was the matter. He didn't even have the decency to tell her, letting her instead find out from his mother! His mother, of all people!

"Why do you have your things?" He walked closer to her, his eyes intent and focused on the clothes she had in her hands.

"Because your *mother* thought it would be best if I didn't share your bed while you 'looked for a mate'!" She kicked the bed. "And I happen to agree with her." She turned around and glared at him. "Why didn't you tell me any of this beforehand? I had to find out from...her."

"I am sorry. I thought you understood." He took the clothes out of her hands.

"Understood what, exactly?" She narrowed her eyes, snatching her clothes back.

He'd never told her he cared for her, never told her he loved her, never pretended there was anything more than sex between them. She did understand. She had taken a little form of affection and built something fictional around the feeling. "I thought you understood that as king I need to find a mate."

"But—"

"Eva, I need a mate who will bring prosperity to Sonis so that it can be a thriving world. I need to help my people be able to provide for themselves."

"So, I don't mean anything to you?" Her chest was on fire. It was going to explode.

"It is not about me or about you. I cannot be so selfish as to only think of myself right now. I have a whole world to think of."

He was right. She had been an easy lay and nothing more, fulfilling her duties as a slave and concubine. He had not promised her anything, so why was she demanding what he had not offered her? She sniffed and picked the rest of her clothes off the bed.

"I need to find a bag. I couldn't find one. I don't want to walk through the halls with my clothes hanging in my arms." *How embarrassing. The tramp walk of shame.*

"Where do you think you are going?"

"I asked Ship to help me. He found an empty apartment for me in the main palace."

"What!" Startled by his sudden outburst, she jumped back. "You will not move out of here!" he said.

"Your mother said I shouldn't stay here. Plus, I can't be here with you while you are making plans to mate with someone else."

"Eva, didn't you hear me? I need to mate with someone who will bring prosperity to Sonis. The match will be in name only. You are mine. You cannot go."

*You mean you won't let me go.*

"You will stay here with me," he said. "When I find a match, we will figure out the rest later."

"No."

"Eva, what would you have me do?"

*Be my protector as you promised.* She lowered her head. "Take me home."

He walked closer to her. "This is your home."

"No, it's not. I want to go home. To Earth." Her chest constricted.

"There's nothing left for you there."

Her eyes met his. "There's nothing for me here either."

"No." He shook his head. "You belong to me."

"You don't own me."

"Yes I do."

She held her clothes tight in her hands. She was leaving. It was no point in arguing with a thick-headed barbarian.

He growled low in his chest as she walked closer to the door, arms full of clothes.

"Taio." She turned her head to look at him. "You may own me on paper, but I will never be your slave."

She turned and left.

# Chapter Sixteen

ഔ

She had almost forgotten what it was like to have a place of her own. Since she'd spent the last few years in a communal living arrangement, the apartment was more than she could have ever dreamed of, one bedroom, a small kitchen and dinette area and a living room with a balcony overlooking a radiant green pond.

Although she enjoyed the privacy of having her own place again, the next few days were long and tiresome. Eva spent all her free time on the training field. With Coyl gone, training with the guards had been easier. Well, first off, there wasn't anyone on the field trying to kill her. She stayed there from dusk to dawn, wearing herself out.

She left the training field only to eat and sleep. The guards even invited her to their private dining hall with them. They even went so far as to start to treat her as one of their own. She would rather eat with them than be forced to watch Taio and the "candidates" ogling each other through the evening meals. Since he was so busy with his guests that he didn't have time to visit the training field, she didn't have to see him at all, really.

During the day, he was out of sight, out of mind. It was during the evening hours that thoughts of Taio crept up. She never imagined the three weeks she had spent with Taio would have this big of an impact. Most of all, there was no one there to stop the nightmares.

While she fought as hard as a man during daylight hours, her nights were spent crying as though she was a girl. By the fourth day, she was kicking herself. She wanted the feel of Taio's arms around her once more.

\* \* \* \* \*

He couldn't stand it! His mother planned everything from the parties to which females would make an acceptable mate. Their ideas of the qualifications of a mate were clearly off. While he wanted to interview every qualified candidate, his mother was pickier. The queen crossed candidates off the list indiscriminately. Ancients forbid if she didn't like the candidate's parents, that offense was an immediate dismissal from the list and the moon.

He had been more than relieved when a message came from the planet Laconia, from a Princess Sa'Mya, who requested an invitation to the festivities. Taio quickly responded with a yes. His mother would be extremely upset, but she needed to be reminded of who was in charge.

"How many females are here?" Rasha approached with Kiehle at his side. They were at one of the many "meet and greets" his mother had arranged.

"Seven, maybe," he replied gruffly.

He spent most of his time "entertaining" his guests. If he wasn't entertaining, he was with his mother, who monopolized the precious time he had left. Eva stayed away from him and when she did come around, she seemed disinterested and distant. She chose instead to spend all of her time training or anywhere else that would put her out of his sight. He came to the conclusion that he missed her.

The human female had crept into his heart. He missed her snoring. He missed the way she slept with her eyes half open. He missed her smart mouth. He missed the way she burrowed beneath the covers when she slept. He missed her body pressed against his at night. He missed her picky food choices. He just plain…missed her.

More times than he would admit publicly, he used the palace's signature heat tracking system to find her whereabouts. His intentions were always to go to her, talk with her or hold her in his arms. He always stopped short, feeling immersed in guilt. He wasn't sure why he should even feel guilty. He needed to figure out what his true feelings for her were before he revealed them to her.

"Is that all? This place is filled with females," Rasha said.

"Not all of them are a suitable match for me. According to my mother, there are only seven females here who will do," Taio said.

Kiehle's eyes scanned the room. "Soooo, you are saying that out of the fifty or so females here, I can have all but seven," he said.

"Eight, you can have all but eight," he quickly added. Both Kiehle and Rasha looked at each other. "What?" Taio asked.

"Nothing," they replied in unison.

"Any prospects so far?" Rasha asked.

"None, they are all incredibly boring. The upside is there will be two more females coming for the party tonight."

Rasha smirked at his friend. "And Eva, what about her? Have you made up with her yet?"

"No. But we will. She is mine. What choice does she have?"

"She could choose to leave and do something else with her time instead of shooting daggers at you from across the room." Rasha nodded his head toward the door.

They all looked across the room to see Eva staring at him with her arms folded across her chest. This was the first time she'd looked at him in two rotations. She clearly was not happy, but she came to see him. At least they were making some headway.

# Chapter Seventeen

ဆာ

When she watched him, Rasha and Kiehle checking out all those other women, she couldn't help but boil over in anger. It took all of her strength to stay rooted in her spot. Her face burned. She tried to guess what they were talking about. She'd avoided him at all costs and the first time she went to him in days, she caught him ogling other women.

Seething in anger, she turned away. He wasn't going to make a fool out of her twice. How stupid was she to seek him out, missing him. Before she reached the hall outside, Taio's strong arms were around her waist, pulling her against him. He leaned down, planting a soft kiss on the nape of her neck, sending shudders down her spine.

"I missed you," Taio said. "Don't go, come with me while I work."

Eva reluctantly let him pull her by the hand to his office. His lavender eyes watched her every move as he settled into his overstuffed office chair.

"Do you need to put yourself on display for those women?" She trailed a hand over one of the elaborate glass statues on the shelf in his office.

"I need to find a good match."

"What will happen to me when you find your mate?"

She couldn't live with this kind of uncertainty any longer. She just recently found some type of normalcy after spending the last three years in hell, it was something she thought about all the time.

Could he easily discard her, even when she still craved to be near him?

"You'll stay with me, of course."

"Stay with you? I don't think your new mate would appreciate me hanging around," she snorted.

"I have told you whatever match I make will be for business purposes only. You are mine, all mine. You will never have to worry about anyone else."

She cocked her head. "You never know. Your new mate might come along and start bossing me around."

"Never. The only bossing would come from me."

"Oh?" She raised her brow. "And what would you tell me to do?"

"For starters, I would have you take my cock in your mouth."

"I think your mate might have some objections to that."

"Not if you shared," he said. "Or she might like watching. You are very good at it."

His dark lashes were framing his smoldering eyes as he watched her move to settle between his legs. He inhaled sharply as she leaned over and ran her tongue over the tattooed claw around his eye. His breathing became ragged as her tongue followed the path down the side of his face and neck, swirling and kissing the entire way. With a soft moan, he closed his beautiful eyes.

She tugged at his shirt, pulling it over his head. His beautiful chest was displayed before her, rising and falling in tight rhythmic movements. His brown nipples were erect, enticing her. Leaning in, she sucked one between her lips. He moaned lightly and clasped her hips, holding her in place as if he were afraid she might leave. She released his nipple and ran her tongue across the intricate pattern on his chiseled chest, feeling every groove in his skin that it made.

Her hand found its way to his powerful cock. She caressed it through his pants. His breaths came out in hard pants as her fingernails scraped the length of it, caressing every thick vein and hard ridge. She slowly dropped to her knees. Her mouth salivated in anticipation.

Tugging on his pants, she finally freed it. She held his gaze as his fingers began to massage the back of her head, urging her forward. She first thought to tease it with her tongue and lips. But Taio had other intentions. He applied slight pressure to the back of her head. There would be no teasing today.

Eva relaxed her jaw as his hand guided her head up and down, slightly pushing her farther down with each stroke. His cock throbbed in her mouth. Her tongue ran across each thick, distended vein. Her eyes fluttered close as she tightened her jaw around his shaft, making her cheeks squeeze him from both sides. Her tongue flattened against his underside and the ridges on the roof of her mouth creating the perfect amount of friction.

Moaning deeply, Taio massaged her head as his scent filled her nose, intoxicating her. Her pussy pulsated and dripped every time his head hit the back of her throat.

Sitting higher on her knees, she angled her head directly over him, wanting to take more. Saliva ran out of her mouth and dripped down his shaft. Using it as a lubricant, she squeezed around the base.

Their earlier conversation coming back to her, she thought of how much of him she couldn't fit in her mouth. *So much to go around.*

"Mmm." She raised her head with a wicked grin. "Maybe you do need a mate. She could help me suck it. You were right, there's enough here for two mouths to share." She playfully licked the pre-cum from his massive head.

With a groan, Taio tangled his fingers in her hair, guiding her mouth back to his throbbing cock. He pressed the intercom with his free hand. "Send Yazmine in," he said in a strained voice.

Eva's body instantly stiffened. It had been a joke. She didn't think he would follow through on her taunt. She stopped sucking and tried to lift her head. She had to stop him.

He held her head firmly in place. "Are you backing down from a challenge?"

Eva paused, unsure if this was a challenge she was willing to meet. She knew he had not been with any other females since she arrived and she didn't think she should open that door.

Reading her uncertainty, Taio brought his hips up. His cock filled her mouth, gliding effortlessly to the back of her throat. Unable to resist the sensation his shaft created, she tightened her cheeks, forcing a groan from Taio.

Eva reached to cradle his big, heavy balls. They were hot and tight in her hand. She milked them down and away from his cock, encouraging them to loosen under her light massage. Taio gripped her head tighter. She smiled, a mere human female from Earth was bringing the warrior king to the edge with her mouth.

The door slid open and shut, followed by light footsteps.

"You called?" a female's voice asked.

Eva recognized Yazmine, although she didn't have many dealings with the tall, beautiful female.

Taio's breaths came out in hard pants. "Eva would like help."

Eager to comply, and without another word, Yazmine dropped to her knees next to her. The beauty watched intently as Eva sucked and licked Taio's cock, eagerly waiting for her turn.

As she greedily worked on his cock, Taio grabbed Yazmine's black- and gold-streaked head, guiding her open mouth to his balls. Yazmine engulfed his balls into her hungry mouth, pulling and tugging on his heavy sac, seemingly to be in a different world, oblivious that Eva worked above her on his cock. Eva's pussy convulsed.

Moaning around his sac, Yazmine flicked her bronze-colored eyes up to Eva. Yazmine's half-closed eyes told of her enjoyment. Letting his sac plop from her mouth, Yazmine turned her head to the side and wrapped her plump lips around the base of his cock. Eva released the suction of her mouth, letting a mouthful of saliva drip down Taio's slippery shaft.

On a lustful moan, she descended down his length, taking as much as she could, meeting Yazmine's mouth. Yazmine released her hold to trail her tongue around Eva's, probing for entry. Eva lifted from Taio's cock and covered Yazmine's mouth with her own. Tasting and exploring her, their tongues entangled, lips pressed against luscious lips.

Eva slid her hand beneath Taio's on Yazmine's head, moving his out of the way. She guided Yazmine's head over Taio's cock. She was immediately impressed with Yazmine's skills. While the girl couldn't take it all, she could take more than Eva. Yazmine sucked and slurped, her plush lips squeezing and working his cock. She pulled his cock from her mouth long enough to fist it, fast and hard, working the pre-cum to the tip, where Eva leaned in and swiped the sweet-tasting liquid off with her tongue.

Taio leaned back in his chair, his face twisted in pleasure. He was only minutes from his breaking point.

Yazmine's mouth clamped down on him again, working at a pace much faster than her own. Yazmine's deep groan vibrated in the back of her throat. Eva watched as the other female sucked her male's cock and, shockingly, enjoyed it. Her pussy was now painfully engorged and wet. She applied more pressure on the back of Yazmine's head, encouraging her to go down farther.

Taio's hands gripped both arm rests, his fingertips digging into the fabric. When she had sucked his cock, did he enjoy it this much? Or was Yazmine just doing a better job? Feeling slightly jealous, Eva plucked Yazmine's mouth off him.

Eva replaced her mouth over his wet cock and mimicked what Yazmine had done. Yazmine moved behind her and began to disrobe. Her prickly pubic hairs were soon pressed against Eva's ass and Yazmine's breasts laid against Eva's back. Eva shuddered.

Kissing her neck, Yazmine reached around and palmed Eva's breasts, massaging them, grinding her hips on Eva's ass. Eva had never thought about being with another female, but she gave in to the moment, pushing her ass back against Yazmine. Yazmine's hand trailed down her stomach, her fingers expertly parting Eva's folds.

Yazmine hesitated, hovering over her clit. "Taio?"

"Human females have clits, Yazmine." His breathing was heavy and hard. "Think of it as a sex bud."

*Sex bud.* That kind of summed it up. Eva pressed her mouth down as far as she could go and moaned onto Taio's cock. Her rhythm increased as her juices dripped down her leg. Yazmine's slender fingers alternated between rubbing her clit and diving into her pussy. Rocking back, she began riding the slender digits.

"May I?" Yazmine asked Taio.

"With my blessing."

Eva didn't have time to wonder what the exchange meant before Yazmine's wet tongue trailed down the curvature of her ass. Shuddering, Eva's fingernails pierced the flesh on Taio's thighs. Yazmine positioned herself under Eva and trailed her tongue up her legs, following the path her dripping juices made. Finally reaching her destination, Yazmine latched on to her swollen clit.

Eva moaned down the length of Taio, his cock tickling the back of her throat. Yazmine wrapped her slender arms around Eva's hips, pulling her deeper onto her face. Eva groaned, the feel of a thick cock in her mouth and a tongue on her clit was more than she could take. Eva lowered her pussy over Yazmine's face, giving Yazmine what she demanded.

Yazmine held Eva's hips firmly to her face, pumping and probing her tongue into her pussy. Taio leaned forward, pushing her head deeper down his cock, pumping his hips, fucking her mouth.

Eva used Yazmine's mouth just as Taio was using hers, her pussy riding Yazmine's strong tongue. Yazmine's grip tightened around her thighs, encouraging her to ride even harder.

Groaning deep, Taio grabbed Eva underneath her shoulders, lifted her up and positioned her over his rock-hard cock. Eva screamed out as Taio impaled her on it without letting her first adjust to his size.

Her pussy suctioned and gripped his cock. The sounds of her slickness filled the room.

Before long, Eva's ass began hitting the top of Yazmine's head every time Taio lowered her down. Reaching back, she felt her helper working his sac, licking and pulling it. Taio grabbed Eva's hips and pounded ferociously into her, spreading her so far apart.

"That's it, I feel it. Come for me," Taio said.

The directive was all Eva needed, her pussy erupting. Roaring, Taio's release followed hers, pumping harder, her tight pussy milking him every inch of the way.

With strong hands, Taio lifted Eva up and around, spreading her legs to straddle his, giving Yazmine easy access to her dripping sheath. Eva yelled out again as Yazmine covered her mouth over her spent pussy, sucking their combined juices from the sweet sheath. Yazmine's hand pumped furiously in her own pussy.

Taio's rough hands palmed and tweaked her nipples. Eva came again as Yazmine sucked and licked, grinding her nose against her clit. Finally, Yazmine let out her own cry as she came, swallowing Eva and Taio's cum.

Eva fell back on Taio as sweat dripped from her body. After a few moments, Yazmine stood up, wiping come off her face with a finger, scooping it into her mouth. Not wasting a drop.

"That will be all," Taio said.

"The pleasure was all mine." Yazmine turned to leave.

Without a doubt, Eva thought.

Her eyes began to droop as she watched Yazmine walk out of the room, surrendering herself to sleep.

# Chapter Eighteen

Taio sat on plush cushions, surrounded by exotic-looking females. The "candidates", as Eva had referred to them. Eva watched as he would lean in to listen to one, occasionally provided another with a smile; one had even elicited a hearty laugh out of him.

She wanted to kick his ass.

The list of many had now dwindled down to nine. She couldn't believe it, nine. Who in the hell needed to surround themselves with nine different females? They flanked him on all sides, literally. They were rubbing his legs, holding on to his arms, rubbing his shoulders, and there was even one standing over him, playing with his hair. And he looked to be enjoying every moment of it.

*I am going to hurt every one of those hussies.*

At first, she tried not to watch the melee in front of her, but they were pretty hard to miss. He sat on his throne, with females falling all over him. *Yuck.* She could feel her eyes getting smaller and smaller with each passing moment.

Luckily for him, the entertainment was beginning and obstructed her view.

"They are from Hisnapal." Eva turned toward the speaker, an extremely handsome male. "They are most renowned for their dance performances. Their skill excels all others in this galaxy."

She remembered he'd arrived the day before with some of the other guests. He stood over six feet tall, with pale skin, gray eyes and nice, lush, pouty lips. His short hair was a silky gray color with shimmering white highlights. Not bad, she thought.

"They are beautiful to watch," she said. She turned back to the show. They were different than anything she had ever seen before. This race had flexible and pliable bones and a body structure that resembled a snake, which made their performance incredible. Their reptilian eyes seemed to entrance the crowd as they moved, bending backward and sideways.

The male settled down on the empty seat next to her. Normally, she would have been uncomfortable with the closeness of a stranger, but seeing how Taio was busy with his fan club, she thought maybe it was time to start her own.

Lo'Ren nudged her in the arm from the other side. Eva turned to her. Lo'Ren's eyes were as large as saucers. With a smile on her lips, she scooted over to allow him ample room to sit comfortably next to her. *Fuck Taio.*

"I am called Alexion Hazouto." He offered her a small dip of his head.

"I am Eva Smith. Nice to meet you, Alexion Hazouto." She returned the gesture.

It was impossible to learn the customs of all the guests, so she figured she would mimic what everyone else did. At least she wouldn't totally stand out and make a fool of herself.

Eva motioned toward Lo'Ren. "This is my friend, Lo'Ren of Briel." Lo'Ren dipped her head as well.

He smiled at them both and then looked at her. "I know who you are," he said. "You are the talk of the palace."

Eva lifted an eyebrow. "Nothing offensive." He chuckled. "I was told you took on two Tresdonians and three royal guards by yourself. Everyone here is quite impressed with your fighting skills."

This time Eva chuckled. "I took the Tresdonians on, but I'm afraid the gossipers may have left out I was beaten to a pulp for my efforts." Alexion's expression turned to confusion. "I did not win," she added.

"One does not have to win in order to be considered a great fighter. Sometimes surviving the fight is all that matters."

She thought about that. Maybe Alexion was right; she had survived, and surviving meant being able to someday reunite with her friend.

"Thank you for your insight. I thought of it as a failure."

"No, quite the opposite, failure would have been death."

"Yes, but it can't be considered a win." *I was still taken away from Ally and made a slave.* She couldn't help thinking that if she would have been conscious, she could have at least asked Taio and Rasha to get Ally as well.

Alexion smiled warmly at her. "Maybe we can call it a draw?"

Eva returned his smile. "I like the sound of that."

Lo'Ren groaned beside her.

There were a few females here who had caught his interest. For all he cared, the other seven could return to their home worlds tomorrow, especially the one raking her hands through his hair. It was making him feel as though he were a pet. He'd removed her hands twice already. Each time, her hands returned and continued on. She definitely would not do, clearly she couldn't follow any type of direction.

One of the two who held his interest was the Princess Sa'Mya from the planet Laconia. A natural sensuality enhanced her beauty. She was the perfect size and height, slender, but curvy. No one would mistake her for a child, another plus.

His gold skin tone paled next to hers. Her hair was a rich gold color that hung loosely down to the small of her back. He thought it was one of her best attributes, along with her sleek legs, and she proudly displayed both. Her speckled, gold-colored eyes added to her beauty.

The other female, Taraj Hazouto, wasn't a princess, but a dignitary from Holis. He was not exactly sure why he considered her. Normally, she wouldn't be his type. She was pretty, unique and interesting, but quiet. She wasn't as tall as the princess, but her pale skin, arresting gray eyes and long silver hair worked for her.

It was only when the dancers from Hisnapal began that he spied Eva across the room, sitting comfortably close to Alexion, Taraj's twin brother. Before he could stop himself, he let a small snarl escape from his throat. The female next to him hastily shifted away. No matter. She was on the "send home" list anyway.

He couldn't make out what the two were discussing, but whatever it was seemed to catch her attention. She actually smiled at him. Eva shouldn't smile at anyone but him! He narrowed his eyes, trying to read their lips. Eva threw her head back and laughed. His chest tightened at that sight.

*I will kill him.*

He launched off his seat, his gaze set on the couple across the room. A firm hand grabbed his arm.

"It may be wiser to stay in place. Your emotional reaction would cause great distress with explanations needed later."

He looked at the hand, then at its owner, Princess Sa'Mya. She was right; stalking across the room to tear apart his lover's admirer would not go well. Unfortunately, his near blunder was witnessed by one of the females he had an interest in.

"Please forgive my actions." He lowered himself down into his seat. *I'll deal with him later.*

"She is a beautiful specimen," Princess Sa'Mya said. "If you want her to stay in the palace after we bond, you will have to work on controlling your emotions in regards to her."

Taio snorted. "You speak as though you are confident I will choose you for the match."

"It seems as though it would be a good match. A match that would be beneficial for us both. You need me and I need you."

He raised an eyebrow. She was bold, maybe too bold for his taste.

"My family owns a transport company in this solar system. The amount of money you could make and save by mating with me would be astronomical. Your gold could reach more markets and at a lower cost. Your moon is lovely, but severely underpopulated. It would be wise to invest in building more homes and social outlets in the unpopulated areas. As I said, you need me."

He mulled over the information she gave him. The ideas of what he could do were already growing in his mind.

"And what do you need from me?" He knew this was too good to be true. If she could offer him all of this, why wasn't she mated already?

"Safety."

# Chapter Nineteen

## ဢ

Eva sat at the dining room table. She planned to first, stuff her face with breakfast and second, work it off on the training field. She was famished, and after spending last night watching Taio and his fan club, she needed to break a few training simulators.

Glancing up, she smiled as Alexion spotted her and made his way over to her. As she watched Alexion, she reminded herself that though her heart belonged to Taio, that male was some kind of eye candy.

"Do you want to go into the village with me?" Alexion asked.

"I haven't been to town yet."

"You've been here long enough to earn a trip to the thriving marketplace." He smiled.

Somehow, she guessed he was making a joke. If the marketplace was thriving, Taio wouldn't have trouble bringing business to his small world.

"I would love to go. But I'm afraid I can't buy anything. I don't have any kind of money…currency…umm…credits."

Ship had tried to explain the monetary system to her before, but it still had her confused. And true to his entity style, he left before the lesson in the universal monetary system was finished. Taio stepped in and explained there wasn't paper money because of the inter-galaxy space travel and trade, so they had a credit system. Since she was new, she had zero credits to her name. Zilch. Not only was she a slave, but she was a very broke slave.

"Come, you will be my guest. It'll be fun." He pulled on her sleeve, leading her out of the room.

"Sure, but I have to check with Taio first."

"Did he forbid you to leave the palace?"

"No, he didn't forbid me to go anywhere." She bristled, she wasn't a prisoner. "But I should still tell him where I am. In case he's looking for me."

"I hardly doubt he will miss you. He is with my sister and the other females at this moment. They are all vying for his attention. Hoping to be the new Queen of Sonis." He exaggerated the last sentence.

Her face instantly fell. Even though she knew what was going on, she really didn't need or want anyone reminding her about it. "So I will inform the pilot that you will be accompanying me to town, yes?" Alexion asked.

"Yes."

When she agreed, she hadn't imagined she would have so much fun traveling to town with Alexion. The small transporter picked them up from the palace steps and dropped them off fifteen minutes later in the epicenter of town.

Eva scrambled from the craft to the almost barren street. Why hadn't Taio taken her to town before? Was it because she was a slave? Not telling Alexion about her slave status made her feel a little guilty. Above anything else, she didn't want him getting into trouble over her.

"Where do you want to start?" He turned to her as the transporter whisked away.

"I don't know." She looked around, suppressing a giggle threatening to escape her lips. A town! Who would have thought she would feel all giddy inside about seeing a town.

"I am but a humble servant at your disposal." Alexion bowed.

"Can we start there?" She pointed to a quaint shop in front of them. The pale-blue awning with the words "Daezal's

Pottery Place" painted across it was as good a place as any to start her exploration.

"After you."

They strolled through the streets, Alexion picking up a few of the local crafts for her. By the afternoon, she had two bags of artwork for her apartment. Whatever the cost, she was going to make it a home.

For lunch, Alexion took her to an outside café where it was easy for her to imagine she was at home at one of the cafés on Main Street. She imagined she and Alexion were sitting at a table, surrounded by other patrons, people watching. Even for that short time, she felt better than she had in years.

By early afternoon, they were exploring the gardens, parks and neighborhoods. The transporter was at their beck and call. It was clear Sonis had a lot to offer and the experience itself was wonderful. For the first time since being taken from Earth, she felt free, as though she could actually build her life here, raise kids and be happy. She would make Sonis work for her.

Alexion was the perfect host, they both acted as the tourists they were. By late afternoon, his sister Taraj joined them.

At first, Eva didn't know how she would feel about Taraj joining them. Technically, she was here to steal Taio away from her. But she was Alexion's twin and she owed it to him to at least be nice to his sister. She could rip out her eyes some other day.

An official royal transporter dropped her off while they were in a fresh foods market.

"Taraj, this is Eva." Alexion led his sister to Eva. She was not going to her. Eva stayed rooted to her spot on the park bench.

"Nice to finally meet you," Taraj greeted her as everyone else had.

Eva didn't immediately return the traditional head nod. She didn't want this female here; she was going to tolerate her because of Alexion. Only after Taraj turned to her brother did Eva finally greet her. Alexion had explained earlier that he and Taraj had special abilities that they both shared. They could sense each other's feelings and read each other's minds, a trait common on their planet.

Late afternoon found Eva and Taraj in a doll shop.

"You love him, don't you?" Taraj asked. Eva looked through the window at Alexion, who had declined to enter. "No, not Alexion. I know you don't love him." Taraj smiled. "I'm talking about Taio."

Should she even be talking about Taio to someone who was technically on Sonis to steal him away?

"Taio? It doesn't matter." Eva shook her head. "I can't give him what he needs. What Sonis needs." She could hear how distant her voice had become. He had told her that statement so many times it was engrained in her.

"Too bad." Taraj picked up a handmade doll and examined it.

"Why?"

"Because he loves you."

Eva snorted. "He doesn't love me. He likes to have sex with me. But he's not in love with me."

Taraj looked at her and tilted her head.

"Don't try to use that Jedi mind trick on me." She laughed, holding her hands up, backing away from the mind reader.

"What's a 'Jedi mind trick'?"

Eva laughed again. "Never mind, you wouldn't understand even if I told you."

Taraj looped her arm through Eva's. "We are going to be friends, you and I."

She could really use a friend right now, she thought, as they walked out of the store arm in arm.

By the time they were on their way back to the palace, she was secretly thinking if Taio had to pick any one, she would like for him to pick Taraj. At least she knew they could be friends.

\* \* \* \* \*

Eva breezed into his office with a radiant glow and it took all his composure not to leap from behind his desk and shake her. Eva had left abruptly with Alexion Hazouto, not even bothering to tell him where she went. Ship told him to give her space, let her keep her apartment, let her "do as she pleased", but leaving the palace walls was unacceptable. Anything could have happened to her while she was trouncing around the city with an off-worlder.

"Where have you been?"

"I went to town with Alexion and his sister Taraj." A burst of energy radiated through her. "We had such a good time. The town was so pretty. It reminded me of one of the small towns that we had in my country on Earth." She plopped down on the corner of his desk.

"It was so wonderful." Homesickness was written all over her face.

Taio reined in his anger, feeling a little guilty for not taking her to town sooner himself. "Did you stop by Holkin's Glass Factory?"

Her eyes widened. "Oh yes, the glassware was beautiful, all the different shapes and sizes. And the colors! I haven't seen any of those colors on Earth."

"I have a lot of his pieces here in the palace. My father was not pleased when Holkin left Drazlan and moved his business to Sonis." He pointed to the large vase on the shelf behind him.

"You have such a wonderful world here, Taio. You need to bring more people here to see it. And children. The parks need children playing in them. What's the plan for that?"

"We don't know why we are unable to breed as other species. It is something my people have worked on for a very long time." He blew out a breath.

"But not for your parents," she said. "They were able to have three children."

Taio gave thought before responding. There had been rumors circulating when Saia was born, but they had since died down.

"My mother and father are much...richer than the average couple. They can afford the best medical advice."

"So if it's such an issue, why can't everyone get the same treatment as your parents did?"

"It is not that easy, not everyone could afford the same medical procedures as my parents. It was very costly."

"On Earth, we bred out of control. If you didn't want to get pregnant, you had to get on some type of birth control."

"Birth control?"

"Yeah. I used to take a little pill every day so I wouldn't get pregnant. And the men have to wear a protective covering over their penises so they won't get the woman pregnant," she explained.

"You could have children, but you didn't want them?"

"It's not the same. I didn't want to get pregnant and not have a way to take care of the baby. You know, without a husband or family. It would be pretty hard for me to raise a kid on my own. If I were married, that would have been a different situation. But I wasn't, so I chose not bring a child into the world with all that uncertainty."

"But I don't understand why people wouldn't want a child if they could have a child."

"Taio, things are different here. If someone had a child on Earth and they didn't want it, they could have aborted it—terminated the pregnancy."

She couldn't be for real. A race that terminated their offspring because of ill-planning?

"Or they could give it up for adoption, you know, give the child away," Eva said.

"I don't believe this!" He slammed his fist on his desk.

"Believe it, I'm living proof." Her voice quivered. "I told you my mother and father didn't want me. I lived in an orphanage all my life with other throwaway kids."

He looked at her surprised. "I thought your parents died. They gave you away?"

"Yes."

While he didn't understand her customs from Earth, he definitely didn't want to cause her any more pain than had already been inflicted on her.

Getting up, he drew her into his arms. "If you were my child, I would have never given you up." He kissed and stroked her head.

"I know."

* * * * *

He spent the entire evening meal watching Alexion and Eva. She was smiling and laughing at everything he said. What was he saying that kept that smile on her face?

"She is a very beautiful female," Taraj said.

Taraj sat on one side of him and Princess Sa'Mya sat on the other. "When are you going to have an enlightenment ceremony for her?"

"An enlightenment ceremony? For Eva?" he asked, bewildered.

141

"Yes, I understand it is a very well-known custom of your race. It seems only natural for Eva to be allowed to participate in the ceremony."

"Females are not warriors. Nor could they ever be seen as such."

Taraj tilted her head. "She battled two Tresdonians and three of your famous royal guards. I think that alone makes her one of the finest warriors in this room."

Taraj's words struck a chord in him. If they were on any world except this one, she would have been recognized as a true warrior a long time ago.

"She seems quite happy with my brother," Taraj said.

"Humph," he replied.

"Don't be sour. It would make us feel inadequate. You are surrounded by some of the wealthiest and prettiest females in the galaxy and all of your attention lies across the room." This remark came from Princess Sa'Mya.

"I'm very pleased to be surrounded by such beauty," he said, trying not to disturb any of his hopeful guests.

Taraj nodded her head, acknowledging his compliment.

Princess Sa'Mya began to talk, about what, he didn't know or maybe he didn't care. She was beautiful to look upon, but he got the feeling she liked to focus mainly on herself. So he let her talk while he watched the pair across the room.

Eva suddenly clapped her hands in glee and leaned over to give Alexion a hug.

*I will kill him.*

He abruptly sat up. His mother put a hand on his shoulder, keeping him in his place. His mother, father, sister and brother had taken the seats on the higher ledge behind him. He let out a low growl that again made the women sitting next to him scoot away.

Kiehle leaned over his shoulder. "Whoa, keep it under control, *brosir*, we don't want to upset any of the females."

"I am in control, Kiehle. I had something in the back of my throat."

"Sure." Kiehle laughed and smacked him on his back.

# Chapter Twenty

ဆ

Eva was completely aware that Taio had kept a jealous eye on her and Alexion last night. Who hadn't noticed it? She had felt his heated gaze from across the room. But what had he expected? He had been surrounded by females who were fawning all over him.

He hadn't seen her running over and drop-kicking them in their faces, had he? No, she had remained composed and enjoyed her dinner with Alexion.

Alexion had been good company. He had given a sympathetic ear when she explained her ordeal with being taken and transported to this galaxy. Not only had he been sympathetic, but he had also come up with ideas for starting a safe haven for humans on different planets. At the mention of his planet possibly being the first safe haven, she had been so happy, she had given him a hug and a kiss on both cheeks.

She would have to get Ship to help her locate any humans in this galaxy and figure out how to get them to Holis. The ideas she and Alexion had begun to come up with had kept them busy throughout dinner. When dinner had been over, they had decided to meet today with Ship and try to come up with some plans.

The morning now found her and Alexion sitting in one of the common rooms, writing down all of their ideas for the new safe haven on Holis. She tossed and turned all night, thinking of what would be needed to put their plan into action.

"Where would we get the credits needed to buy them?" Eva asked. The Tresdonians had given her to Taio, but she didn't expect any of the other humans to be free.

"Don't worry about it. Taraj is a dignitary; she'll be able to take care of it. She can work on getting humans declared an endangered species or she can find a donor to put up the credits we would need to buy them."

Heavy footsteps stopped abruptly at the door. A familiar heat caressed her body. Taio was here.

"Come join us." She waved him over. His face was set in a hard scowl. *What's his deal now?*

Without saying a word, Taio walked past her and punched Alexion hard in the face. The loud crack of bone against bone bounced off the walls.

She sat in stunned disbelief as Taio grabbed the front of Alexion's shirt, snatching the half-dazed man off the floor. With a flick of the wrist, Taio sent him flying across the room.

She snapped back to reality. "Taio! Stop!"

Taio unsheathed his *jango*, his eyes fixed with a deadly stare. After hitting the floor with a heavy thud, Alexion quickly recovered from the unprovoked attack and jumped up into a fighting stance. Alexion looked almost as deadly as Taio.

"Are you taking up for this male?" Taio demanded.

"Yes!"

"Eva, I don't need you to protect me, I'm perfectly capable of defending myself," Alexion said, still in battle stance.

"Why do you protect him?" Taio yelled. His murderous gaze shifted from Alexion to Eva, then back again.

"Don't yell at her!" Alexion said.

Taio let out a low growl and stepped toward Alexion again. Alexion widened his stance, waiting for his opponent.

"I said stop! Now! This is so ridiculous," she said.

"What I find ridiculous is a male who intends to keep you under lock and key while he is actively looking for a mate," replied Alexion. Well, in truth, Eva thought it was ridiculous as well. "You would be enough for me, Eva, there wouldn't be a reason to find another."

Eva blinked twice. That was the best sort-of-proposal she'd ever gotten.

"You will not have her!" Taio ran toward Alexion. Alexion held his ground and tried to step out of the way. Taio, almost missing him, flung the *jango* out and caught Alexion on the knees. Alexion cried out in pain, grabbing his knees as he went down.

Eva sprinted over and jumped on Taio's back as he went for Alexion again. "Are you crazy? You have to leave him alone."

"Why do you continue to protect him?" Taio asked, bewildered.

"Because he's my friend, I like him. The same way I like Rasha."

"The way you like Rasha?" he asked questioningly.

She clung to his back. "Yes!"

"I like you as more than a friend," Alexion said. He was on the ground, rubbing his knees.

"Be quiet, Alexion! Before he kills you."

* * * * *

Sa'Mya relaxed in one of the lounge chairs provided on the balcony off her royal suite. She guessed from its size, the balcony was meant to hold ten to fifteen people comfortably. The balcony offered an unobstructed view of the training field, probably for guests to watch the elite royal guards train. The balcony's canopy provided enough shade from the suns, allowing her to sit in comfort to watch the human female.

*Why did Taio allow his concubine to train with the males?*

The small patter of feet approached her. She turned her gaze from the training field to Moira, her personal assistant.

"Princess, your uncle has requested you contact him immediately," Moira said.

Moira had come from one of the small villages outside the capital city. Despite her looks, Moira wasn't much older than herself. Many cycles of hard work in the factory, making parts for transporter vessels, had left the female with a hard disposition and haggard appearance. The fine dress and easier lifestyle she now enjoyed did little to cover up the effects of her earlier life.

"Did you tell him I was busy?" Sa'Mya turned back to watch the human female with her personalized *jango*. *Why would she want to behave as a male?*

"Yes, Princess, I told him you were busy. I've told him that for the last two rotations."

Sa'Mya was in trouble, she had to come up with a plan. And fast. Nebin, her loyal guard, had been with her since birth, originally appointed by her now deceased parents. If her uncle caught her, he would surely take her personal assistant and guard away. Moira, although she had grown fond of her, was replaceable. Nebin was not.

"Contact him. Taraj and Alexion Hazouto are leaving this evening, tell my uncle we are accompanying them to Holis." Sa'Mya was sure she needed just a little more time to procure a bonding contract.

"And when he finds out we have not left Sonis?" Nebin asked, his baritone voice breaking his silence.

Nebin stood by her side, even though she had offered him a seat across from her. Her guard intimidated all who gazed on him. He even towered over many of the warriors on Sonis. His arresting light-gray eyes were a sharp contrast against his dark-colored skin. His appearance was enough to make anyone who wished her harm to take pause, but his loyalty stopped them in their tracks.

"Don't worry about that. We will soon have the protection of King Taio. I expect a proposal from him before my uncle realizes that we have not left Sonis."

Sa'Mya watched the training field again. Eva was a minor distraction. Sa'Mya's error had been waiting for Taio to seek her out for a proposal. An error she would need to correct now.

Sa'Mya didn't waste any time looking for Taio.

"May I please disturb you?" Sa'Mya walked into his office, accompanied by Moira and Nebin. Sa'Mya sat down in the empty seat next to Rasha, not waiting for an invitation.

"I guess I have no choice in the matter," Taio said.

Ignoring his retort, Sa'Mya pressed on, afraid if she stopped to think about what she was doing, she would lose her nerve. She needed this too badly.

"Are you aware of Mercanis Shipping and Hauling?" she asked.

"Everyone as far as the next two galaxies has heard of Mercanis Shipping and Hauling."

"So you are aware it is the largest and most profitable transport company in this galaxy and it continues to grow with each passing year."

Taio leaned back in his chair, crossing his arms at his chest.

"Well, I am the sole owner of the company," Sa'Mya said.

Rasha let out a loud breath.

Taio lifted a brow. "You expect me to believe you own Mercanis Shipping and Hauling. You aren't even capable of dressing yourself."

Sa'Mya lifted her chin higher at the dig. "An ancestor founded the company before I was born. The company has since passed down to my father. After he and my mother died, my uncle took over the day-to-day operations of it, but I am the sole owner of the company. I inherited it."

Rasha choked again. Taio leaned closer to his desk. "And this information means what to me?"

She leaned closer to him. "It means if we bond, not only will you be part owner of the company, but you will also have the entire company at your disposal. Are you interested?"

Taio leaned back in his chair. "I am interested," he finally said. "What are the conditions of your proposal?"

"We bond."

Taio snorted. "I assumed a match was in order. But what else do you want?"

"I want the bonding ceremony to happen immediately."

"How soon is immediately?" he asked, hesitating slightly.

"Today, before you leave for Holis."

Rasha choked again. Both Sa'Mya and Taio looked at him. "Sorry" was all he could say.

"Although my mother would love for me to bond today, it would be impossible. We have to make preparations and draw up the proposal contract."

"Tomorrow will be fine." The sooner she was bonded, the sooner she could claim her rightful place on her planet.

Taio steepled his fingers together and looked intently at her. "It will take place in seven rotations. I have to escort Taraj and Alexion Hazouto back to Holis and take care of some business. When I return, we can have one rotation for our traditional festival before the bonding ceremony. Is that acceptable to you?"

Sa'Mya looked at her guard. Seven rotations. Would she be able to hold her uncle at bay for that long? What if he found out she was not on the transport to Holis as well? Would she come to Sonis looking for her?

If her uncle got to her before she bonded with Taio, this would all have been for naught. But this was the closest she'd ever come to total freedom.

"I accept."

"Very good. I will make the announcement before I leave."

"No!" Sa'Mya jumped out of her seat. Catching herself, she sat back down. "I want it to be kept as quiet as possible until the day of the bonding ceremony."

"Why?" he asked.

"I have my reasons. We have a deal as long as you don't send out off-world announcements."

"Deal."


Alone in his office, he struggled to find a way to tell Eva about his upcoming bond to Princess Sa'Mya. They both knew this day would eventually come, but neither had planned it would be this soon. Eva just had to understand this was exactly what Sonis needed.

Why hadn't anyone told him the princess owned Mercanis Shipping and Hauling? She had said something or another about a business earlier, but he had paid her no mind. He would kill Ship.

He'd asked Ship to perform a background check on all of the females in attendance. Ship hadn't brought him any information of this magnitude. He would definitely have to bring it up with him later. The entity probably hadn't told him in hopes that Taio would allow the princess to leave and eventually bond with Eva. His longtime friend's priorities were not in the right place.

"Ship," Taio called out.

"I'm here," the entity replied.

"Where is Eva?"

There was a slight pause while Ship located Eva's heat signature on the palace grounds.

"She is in Taraj and Alexion Hazouto's guest apartment." The news didn't sit well with him. Would he have to beat that male again? Didn't he know to stay away from Eva?

"Ship, where is Taraj and where is Alexion?" He could feel his anger mounting. Heat radiated from his neck to his face. The hairs on the back of his neck stood on end.

"Taraj is in the gardens with Lo'Ren and Alexion is in his guest apartment with Eva."

They were alone? Taio's stride increased as he made his way toward the palace guest apartments. His fists flexed and clenched the entire way. Galactic Council or not, he was going to kill Alexion.

As he turned the corner, the apartment door slid open. Taio slowed his pursuit. Eva was backing out, talking to an unknown person.

"I will miss talking with you," Taio overheard her saying. Then a distant muffled sound came from the other side of the door.

"And you will contact me and keep me updated?" More muffles. "You are the best, Alexion, truly. I don't know what I would do without you." Alexion stepped out of the apartment and Eva hugged him.

Taio watched as his female hugged another male. A male she claimed to like as a "friend". Blood drained from his face as he turned on his heel. He would never let a female make a fool out of him. Maybe Rasha was right, Eva wouldn't be able to continue a relationship with him as things stood. He headed straight to his personal quarters, where he packed a small bag for the short trip.

"Ship, inform Taraj and Alexion Hazouto I am ready for departure." He stalked to the transporter that would take him to the *Saia II*.

"Should I give them a reason as to why you wish to depart before the scheduled time?"

"No."

"What information shall I pass on to Eva?"

"Tell Eva she is to serve Princess Sa'Mya while I am away."

There was a slight pang in his heart as he gave the directive, but as fast as it came, it quickly went away. She was not a real slave and he had never treated her as one. But he gave her his best and she chose another over him.

Hopping in his transport, he punched the control panel, activating the takeoff sequence. Alexion and Taraj could take another transporter to the *Saia II*. He definitely didn't trust himself to be in close quarters with Alexion without killing him.

# Chapter Twenty-One

**ഇ**

Eva asked Ship to repeat himself a couple of times before Taio's message finally sank in. She was meant to be the princess's personal slave. Her chest pains hadn't subsided since. Taio had never treated her as if she were a slave.

Until now.

He'd promised to take care of her. Was this how he intended to do it? Lending her out as a personal slave to this bitch? If he could do this, how would he treat her after he found a mate?

This hurt, literally hurt. Her first thought was to call and let him know exactly how she felt about his directive. *Go to hell.* But she couldn't get past the pain. She wasn't even sure she would be able to hold a decent conversation with him right now.

Taio hadn't been gone for more than a few hours before Princess Sa'Mya started issuing orders. Eva had spent the past few rotations obliging every wish and whim, from foot massages to cleaning the bitch's teeth. Whenever Eva balked, the princess called over a waiting guard. All of whom had gotten the directive as well—Eva was to serve Princess Sa'Mya.

Eva bided her time in servitude, fuming. Taio would definitely pay for this. Nothing could make up for the humiliation she was feeling, especially right now. Since the bitch princess apparently didn't know how to wash herself, Eva had to. Eva sat on the ledge, naked, running a brush through Sa'Mya's now clean hair.

*This is just until Taio returns*, she thought with each downward stroke.

"I wonder what he sees in you," Sa'Mya said. She leisurely skimmed the water's surface with her fingertips. Recognizing a rhetorical question when she heard one, Eva didn't respond. "I am offering him all of this." Sa'Mya ran her wet hands down her voluptuous body.

Her double-D breasts hung ripe and full. Her neatly tapered waist led to full-sized hips, a round ass and, of course, long, shapely legs.

"You have the body of a child," Sa'Mya sneered.

*I could apply a small amount of pressure to her windpipe.* Clearly the princess didn't know anything about fighting. Talking smack while your back is to an opponent was a no-no.

"It's clear he can't keep his hands off you. I smell your scent on him every time he comes near me. Gads. When does he not have his cock in you?"

Eva chuckled. That was her intent, to mark Taio with her scent, hoping all the other females would get the idea and go home.

Sa'Mya whipped her head around to face Eva. "Let's see who'll have the last laugh when I bond with him." Sa'Mya smiled. "I think I'll give you to the guards, to do with as they please."

Eva straightened on the ledge. "He'll never share me with anyone else." Eva met her eye for eye.

Taio definitely was not the sharing type. He nearly caused a war between Sonis and Holis just because he thought she liked Alexion. No, there wouldn't be any passing around, Taio would rip any male to shreds who thought to touch her.

"You think not?"

Sa'Mya pushed off the ledge with a malicious smile across her lips.

She turned around to stare at Eva. "You'll never be able to compete with me."

"I'm not trying to compete with you." *Bitch.*

Sa'Mya took a step closer, her eyes downcast.

"What does he find so interesting down there?"

Eva snapped her knees together.

"Let me see," Sa'Mya demanded.

"No." Eva swung her legs around to propel herself to a standing position.

"Make one more move and I'll have you taken to the guards right now."

Eva stopped, her legs propped on the ledge. "Taio wouldn't let you." But unfortunately he wasn't here right now.

"Of course." Sa'Mya tilted her head. "He would be upset if his precious royal guards ran through his pet." She shrugged. "But then the damage would have already been done. Wouldn't it?"

Sa'Mya's unblinking, gold-speckled eyes rested on her.

Eva froze.

This bitch was crazy enough to follow through on her threat. Eva wasn't worried that the guards would rape her. She would kill anyone who tried. It was Taio she worried about. She didn't want to cause any more trouble between her and the guards. Eva lowered back onto the ledge, dangling her legs in the water.

Sa'Mya sauntered forward until she was standing in front of Eva, putting a hand on her knees. She pried her legs open slightly. Sa'Mya squinted and focused on the nest of dark curls.

"It looks normal. Is there something about it that would appeal to him more?"

Another rhetorical question, Eva kept her mouth shut. Sa'Mya trailed her hand from Eva's knees to her folds, parting them with two fingers.

"What exactly are you looking for? If you haven't noticed, I'm a female."

Sa'Mya ignored her. "What is this?" Sa'Mya pointed to her nub that jutted out from between her exposed folds.

"It's called a clit."

"What does it do?" Sa'Mya placed a finger on it.

Startled, Eva jumped. "It doesn't *do* anything." She flicked Sa'Mya's finger out of the way. "All human females have one, it enhances sexual feelings."

"I want a better look. Spread your legs wider."

"They're wide enough," Eva ground out. She had as much as she was taking from the bitch princess. The inspection was more extensive than Taio's.

Sa'Mya dug her nails into the skin of Eva's knees. "Either you can open them or I'll have one of the guards hold your legs open for me."

Eva thought about it for a second. This was embarrassing enough. *Oh how I want to kill this bitch.*

"When Taio left me in your care, I highly doubt this was what he had in mind," she said.

Sa'Mya's nails dug deeper into her flesh. "Take it up with Taio when he returns."

*Oh and I will.* She opened her legs.

Sa'Mya smiled triumphantly. "A clit, you said? What an odd name." Sa'Mya inspected the little nub. "How does it 'enhance sexual feelings'?" The tip of Sa'Mya's finger ran across the nub again.

"Nerves, it's got nerves in it," Eva said through clenched teeth. "And it's very sensitive."

Sa'Mya pointed and eyed Eva's slit, tilting her head to the side. "Look there, such a tiny opening for such a large male. When he fucks you, does it hurt?"

Surprised, Eva asked, "Have you ever been with a male before?"

Sa'Mya closed her eyes. "Slave, did I give you permission to ask me questions?"

*I am going to kick this bitch's ass.*

Opening them again, Sa'Mya slid her thumb inside Eva's sheath.

Eva jumped back. "You've gone too far. What do you think you're doing?"

"I want to know what makes you so special." Sa'Mya leaned in closer and pushed her thumb deeper inside. "This is too tight. He must be huge, how does it fit in here?"

*Nope. This nut is definitely a virgin.*

"It just does."

Satisfied with her probing, Sa'Mya put her hands on Eva's knees, spreading them wider. She kneeled on the submerged bath bench, her nose inches from Eva's pussy.

Sa'Mya leaned in closer and inhaled sharply. "Maybe he's attracted to the smell. It is quite intoxicating."

Sa'Mya had spent the better part of the day using her. So she shouldn't feel guilty about what she was about to say.

"He likes the taste." *Nope, no guilt at all.*

"What did you say?"

Eva cleared her throat. "I said he particularly likes the taste. He can't get enough of licking and sucking my clit."

Sa'Mya peered up through squinted eyes. "You lie."

Eva shook her head. "No, every chance he gets, he's got his head buried between my legs." Eva adjusted herself better on the ledge, tilting her mound slightly upward.

"How does it taste?"

"He claims it's the best delicacy he has ever tasted." She tried her best to mimic a chef from one of those old Earth cooking shows.

"Interesting." Sa'Mya pulled her bottom lip between her teeth and inched closer. Sa'Mya's hot breath lingered on her clit. She stuck out her tongue, giving the nub a quick lick. Eva caught her breath.

"Not bad." Two more licks followed.

A small moan escaped Eva's lips. There was something oh so wrong about all of this, but she didn't care. Eva opened her knees wider, inching her butt closer to the ledge.

Eva wanted to hold the princess's head closer to her pussy, but she didn't dare, afraid it might cause her to stop. Instead, Eva put her hands on her trembling thighs, holding them open, and watched. Sa'Mya explored her clit with her tongue, first darting, then licking, before finally pulling it into her mouth and sucking.

Sighing, Eva leaned back on her elbows on the cool, tiled floor. Sa'Mya's hands gripped her thighs hard, forcing her legs open even wider. There was no resistance from Eva. She was no Yazmine, but she would do.

Sa'Mya's soft tongue swiped from her slick opening to her clit, repeating each lick a little harder than the first. A deep, lustful moan followed after each swipe.

Eva moaned in time with Sa'Mya, a slight wiggle in her hips adding to the pleasure. Her eyes rolled back with the thought of running her fingers through Sa'Mya's hair, itching to push her in deeper.

Slow and tentative, Sa'Mya's tongue probed deep in her dripping sheath, exploring and massaging her walls. Eva let out a groan and threw her head back. Sa'Mya's tongue darted in and out. Eva's stomach quivered and her legs shook.

Sa'Mya wrapped her arms around Eva's thighs, holding on tight, and tongue-fucked her in slow strokes. Eva raised her head long enough to watch Sa'Mya's golden head bob between her legs.

*Good gracious.*

Her wall gripped at Sa'Mya's exploring tongue. Eva's breathing increased to a feverish pitch as she reached to rub her throbbing nub.

Eva's wet fingers glided over her sensitive bud, rubbing in slow circular motions. Sa'Mya spread her folds farther apart, kissing, licking and probing the slick slit that she had begun to enjoy. Sa'Mya left her slickness twice to swipe a hot, wet tongue across Eva's fingers and clit before dipping back inside.

Eva's stomach quivered more as she listened to the princess's greedy moans. Eva's pace quickened, her fingers rubbed her clit vigorously. She needed release.

With a groan, and unable to stop herself, Eva reached down and held the princess's head in place, bringing her hips up to buck against it. Sa'Mya didn't try to pull away, but went in deeper and harder, moaning more as her tongue pulsated in and out as fast as she could.

Sa'Mya pulled back momentarily, licked her lips and watched the juices drip from Eva's cunt. A small mew of complaint crossed Eva's lips. Sa'Mya obliged by wrapping her arms around Eva's thighs, diving back in hard and fast.

Eva tightened her thighs around Sa'Mya's head and erupted, shaking to her core. There was something about having the bitch princess licking her pussy that made Eva want to come all over her.

"Lick it all," Eva whispered.

Sa'Mya cupped her mouth over Eva's slit and lapped.

Sa'Mya finished the last drop. "Turn around."

Although spent, Eva did as she was instructed. She willed her tired body to roll onto her stomach.

Sa'Mya's hands bit into her waist, forcefully pulling her closer. Eva's stomach slid across the floor until her ass was propped up by the ledge and her knees rested on the bath bench below. Soft hands palmed her ass as hard teeth scraped across it. Quivering, Eva pressed her face against the cool floor.

Sa'Mya kneaded one cheek and smacked the other.

Eva raised her head with a start. "Wha...?" The pain radiated from her ass to her pussy, causing it to contract involuntarily.

"I bet you don't listen to him at all." Sa'Mya took another painful nip at her cheek.

Against her will, Eva's head fell back to the floor. "Yes I do."

*Smack.* "You are such a little liar."

Eva inhaled sharply. Her ass was on fire. She should put up a fight, but the contractions in her pussy held her in place. Sa'Mya reached down and kissed the spot she just hit. Eva's pussy convulsed again.

"I have seen the disrespectful looks you give him." Sa'Mya leaned down and swiped a long, wet tongue across her cheek. "Why do you disrespect him in front of his people?"

Eva's fingers gripped at the hard floor. Her nipples painfully hardened. "I don't disrespect him."

*Smack.* Sa'Mya hit her directly on the spot she had licked. "Are you calling me a liar now?"

Juices dripped down her inner thigh. She closed her eyes. She didn't know if she should say yes or no. Never had she been into S&M, but her pussy was getting wetter by the second.

"Yes."

*Smack. Smack.* The sound of Sa'Mya's palm hitting her ass reverberated off the walls. "I am a princess. He is your king. Neither of us will tolerate your insubordination!" *Smack.*

Eva moaned from both pain and pleasure. A tear slipped from her eye as she quivered and dug her fingernails across the tiles, hating the bitch princess for making her feel this way.

Sa'Mya scraped long fingernails down the length of Eva's ass. Then she followed the trail with her tongue, causing Eva to throw back her head. She wanted to come, needed to come.

Sa'Mya grazed a finger over Eva's ass. "What of this one? Do you let him fuck you here as well?"

"No. He would rip me apart."

"Good. This will be just mine." Sa'Mya's tongue pressed against the tight opening.

Eva yelled out as Sa'Mya's hands gripped her ass cheeks, holding them farther apart. Sa'Mya's tongue breached the tight opening.

Sa'Mya's tongue slowly filled her up. Eva relaxed against it, allowing Sa'Mya to go as deep as she wanted. Instinctively, she slowly rocked back, encouraging her to go deeper.

She pressed her chest to the ground, her hot nipples feeling good against the cold tile. Eva groaned, the thought of the biggest bitch in the galaxy with her face buried in her ass was enough to send her over the edge.

The familiar buildup approached fast, her knees shook uncontrollably. Reaching down, she rubbed her clit hard and fast. Sa'Mya's fingers covered hers, rubbing in unison.

"I'm going to come!"

Sa'Mya moved under Eva's pussy to lap at her dripping cunt.

Eva shuddered as Sa'Mya drank, licked, then probed her pussy, as if she didn't believe Eva was finished and looked for more. Eva shuddered again before falling flat.

"Maybe I'll keep you around after all," Sa'Mya murmured. "But know this, the moment I tire of you, I will give you to the guards."

Sa'Mya climbed out of the bath and her soft footsteps walked away.

Eva didn't want anything more than to knock her in her face. She wouldn't spend another minute playing personal slave or sex slave.

# Chapter Twenty-Two

## ୫୬

Eva tapped her fingernails on her teeth, sitting in the overstuffed office chair watching the console on Taio's desk.

"Ship, can you explain it to me again?" She squinted at the computer-generated simulation of the rotation of Sonis around the dual suns.

"For every rotation that passes on Sonis, one and a half rotations have passed on Earth. What you would consider a standard Earth month would equal to twenty rotations on Sonis." Ship's reply was dry and tired—this was the fifth time he'd repeated himself.

"Soooo… I've been on Sonis for about forty-two rotations." Eva used her fingers as a guide. "It would have been sixty-three days or rotations on Earth?" she asked.

"That is correct." His tone still sounded bored. He'd tried to explain this to her for the past half hour or was it one Earth hour? Argh!

After waking up this morning and vomiting all over the place, stress was the first thought that crossed her mind. Then she thought it had something to do with the food she had eaten the night before. It could have been anything but this.

*I'm pregnant.*

Her last period had been about a month before even coming to Sonis. Before that, it had been sporadic at best. She knew that because of high amounts of stress, it wasn't uncommon not to get a period for months at a time. But there was no mistaking it. She was pregnant by Taio.

She'd noticed that her stomach was getting a slight bulge to it and had tried to work it down. There was no way she was going to have a potbelly with all these females walking around, vying for her man's attention. Screw that.

So every day she killed herself doing crunches, to no avail. Now the morning sickness had kicked in. How far along was she? She couldn't even be sure. Maybe somewhere between one and a half to two months?

*What is a typical gestation for these people?*

*Oh my God! How huge is this baby going to be?*

Taio.

How would he even react? Maybe he would react well to the news? Maybe he would keep her and the baby here in the palace with him? Would he still find another mate? Would he be able to bond with her after finding out about the pregnancy? Could he even acknowledge the baby?

She was officially freaking out.

"There is no need to worry, Eva," Ship said. "Taio will be more than pleased about the pregnancy."

"Are you sure?" Her voice quivered.

"I am positive. He has long since given up the idea of a traditional birth. He will be pleased."

She rubbed her belly. *My baby will be loved.* "What about me?" Even if Taio claimed the baby, what would become of her?

"You now carry the one thing he has dreamed about. An offspring. A means and way to populate Sonis."

Her anxiety melted away. Taio talked about it nonstop. He needed to make Sonis a thriving world. What better way than an heir?

"Shall I connect him to you?"

Although it wouldn't take more than a few minutes for Ship to establish a link between her communication console and Taio's on the *Saia II*, she decided against it. She wanted to tell him, but she would wait until he came back from Holis. This was definitely face-to-face news.

"No, I'll tell him tonight." She smiled. She was going to be a "baby mama".

She definitely had a lot on her mind. She was at the only place that would make her feel better, the training field. Eva sat on the sandy ground near the field, polishing her *jango*. It really didn't need polishing, the weapon already shone so bright that colored speckled lights danced off it. It was just something to do as she watched the guards train and enjoyed the suns high in the sky. Luckily for her, she didn't have to wear the sun-resistant blanket anymore, her skin having growing accustomed to the harsh heat as the days passed.

The suns were bright, that was for sure. But the wind blowing off the Singha Ocean, the only ocean on Sonis, was a welcome relief. She hadn't been there yet, but Taio promised to take her one day. Maybe he would take her before the baby was born?

Multiple footsteps came up behind her. Turning around, she watched as Princess Sa'Mya sauntered up to her with her personal guard and assistant in tow.

"I am surprised to see you sitting away from all of the barbaric activities known as training."

Could she never get away from this chick? She'd spent the entire morning at the princess's beck and call. Her only reprieve was when she finally introduced Sa'Mya to Yazmine. Only then was she finally able to escape for a private moment with Ship. She came to the training field to work her twisted muscles. With Taio set to come back soon, her nerves were shot.

"It looks as though I won't need to travel far for a good fight, one is coming right at me," Eva snarled.

Sa'Mya's guard placed a hand on the blaster hanging on the side of his hip. The princess put a hand on his, stopping him.

Eva chuckled. Sa'Mya's assistant placed a blanket on the ground next to Eva, which Sa'Mya slowly lowered herself onto.

"Well, this is somewhat...cozy." Sa'Mya looked around, as if it were beneath her to sit on the ground.

"No one made you come out here and certainly no one asked you to sit down."

"I am aware that you do not like me, Eva."

Eva cut her eyes at Sa'Mya. Whatever would have given the princess that crazy idea?

"I think it would be best for us to get along or try to under the circumstances," Sa'Mya said.

*I don't like the sound of that.* "What circumstances?"

"Master and servant, of course."

Eva inhaled a deep breath, trying to remain calm. "I am no one's servant. And you are no one's master."

"It seems you have forgotten already. Taio left a directive that you are to serve me in his absence. When we bond, I expect the arrangement will be much the same."

"I'm pretty sure it was a mistake, one he'll straighten out when he returns." Her hands gripped her *jango* tightly.

Sa'Mya chuckled. "What do you think your role will be here once he and I bond?"

"I already told you. He won't bond with you." She looked the princess up and down. "You're not his type."

"My type, his type." She flicked out her hand dismissively. "That hardly matters. What matters is what I can do for this little moon and what he can do for me."

Eva looked away from her. Taio had told her countless times, the arrangement would be in name only. Please, anyone but the bitch princess, she prayed.

"Things have changed," Eva said. *I'm going to have his baby.*

"Whatever makes you feel better, human. I am rather looking forward to our business arrangement with," she looked Eva up and down, "*perks.*"

Eva stood up. "Forget it, bitch. I'm speaking to Taio as soon as he gets back. If you need company, go find Yazmine, she'll be more than happy to take care of you."

"Think about it, Eva. Taraj Hazouto has gone back home and I am the only one left. It is inevitable that he and I will bond."

"He told me he wanted to search some more before making a decision. Why settle for you? He's in no rush, especially since he has me in his bed."

Sa'Mya dipped her head slightly. "I am aware he buries himself in you night and day. That is why I thought we should come to some type of reconciliation. You will have to show me respect if you want to continue to bed my mate. Otherwise, you could come to some type of unfortunate accident." Sa'Mya shrugged and looked toward her guard.

Eva didn't flinch from her obvious threat. Taio would never let Sa'Mya harm her in any way, especially now that she carried his child.

"Threaten me again, *Princess,* and I'll cleave your tongue out with the first thing I find. And then for good measure, I'll poke holes in your eyes. I will leave you unable to threaten anyone else ever again. *Mistress.*"

Before her guard could reach for his blaster again, she left to join the guards. *That bitch can sure make anyone want to pummel her into the ground,* she fumed as she walked away from the trio.

Sa'Mya watched Eva walk away. The conversation had gone better than she thought it would. Eva was wrong, of course. Taio would not resume his search for a mate. Sa'Mya wouldn't return to her home world without the protection of King Taio.

He did spend much of his time fucking Eva. It should bother her, but it didn't. She had never been with a male before and was not sure if she ever wanted to be with one. So if Taio fucked Eva, it meant he wouldn't expect the same treatment from her.

She wanted Eva to stay to fulfill those needs for him, but she also wanted them both to tone it down after the bonding ceremony. Even if she didn't want to have sex with her mate, she didn't want the rest of the palace to know it was still going on.

She would have to speak with Eva again, this time forming her words better so Eva wouldn't walk away before she got her point across.

She watched as Eva finally reached the training field and began to swing at the structures, undoubtedly wishing it was her she was beating. She had been truthful when she told Eva she understood why Taio kept his head between her legs. Eva was a fine specimen.

"Find the servant Yazmine and have her meet me in my chambers," she said to Moira.

Sa'Mya smiled as she listened to her assistant carrying out the order. Yazmine would keep her busy until Taio arrived.

# Chapter Twenty-Three

**ဢ**

"It is my honor to introduce you to my chosen mate, Princess Sa'Mya." Taio wrapped his arm around Sa'Mya's shoulders. They both exchanged a smile as the room erupted in cheers and hollers. Everyone around her was ecstatic.

Eva plastered a smile across her quivering lips.

*What did I expect?*

*Commitment?*

*Love?*

*Forever?*

*Marriage?*

*Wife?*

*Husband?*

*Family?*

She was clearly the fool, again.

The only fool in the room.

The only fool who believed an orphan from Earth could be wanted by the King of Sonis.

An elephant sat on her chest. Pain radiated from her jaw down to her left shoulder and arm. The room was getting dimmer.

*Good Lord. I'm having a heart attack.*

Lo'Ren approached her.

*What the hell is she talking about?*

Was she asking her if she was okay? For real?

Her entire world, being, had come crashing around her.

*Why does she have that look on her face?*

She tried to smile harder for Lo'Ren, wanting the other female to see she was fine and leave her alone.

She took a wild sweeping glance around the room. Who the hell was turning down all the lights? And who turned up the heat, sheesh. She was on fire.

Her eyes swept to Taio and Sa'Mya again. Sa'Mya was smiling broadly at Taio's mother and sister while he stood by her side, his arm now around her waist.

*The fucker. Son-of-a-bitch cocksucker.*

Her fingers began to tingle.

Oh yes, she had almost forgotten she was having a heart attack.

"Excuse me, Lo'Ren. I think I may be having a heart attack. I don't want to embarrass myself any more than I have, so I'm going to leave now." She turned and made her way toward the exit.

Smiling at everyone she passed.

Lips still quivering and eyes misting over.

She walked down the corridor, picking up her pace the farther she got away from the reception room. She started for her apartment but stopped short.

"I have nowhere to go," she whispered. She stood in place for a little longer as the realization hit her.

She didn't want to go back to her apartment. The apartment that belonged to Taio.

She turned in the opposite direction, toward the training field. Only after reaching the dark and deserted training field did she allow herself to crumble. She had endured loss and abandonment before, being alone and being unwanted. She would get through this as well.

But right now it hurt.

\* \* \* \* \*

Opening her eyes, she stared at the dusty ceiling. It was familiar to her, as it should have been. She had looked at the same rain spot for what seemed like forever.

She let her eyes focus on the right corner, where a green-and-orange-spotted spider had its web. She had never seen a spider that big, that orange, that hairy or that ugly before. At first she had been afraid of it. Then she began to welcome its bite, hoping it was deadly and quick. Now she realized it was just a fat, ugly, lazy spider.

She did feel somewhat better. She no longer wanted to lie in the equipment room and die. This was her first pity party and hopefully her last. If Taio didn't want her, then fine. He was not the first person who rejected her, but he would surely be the last.

She was so much stronger than this. There'd been walls in place to prevent this sort of thing. Whose idea was it to let them down anyway?

Rolling to a sitting position on the side of the training mat, she let her feet hit the floor. Her head immediately dropped to her hands and arms to her knees. She was exhausted. She only moved to empty her bladder. She'd cried herself dry.

Time to get up and get on with her life. With or without Taio.

"You have decided to get up now?"

Although he had not spoken to her, she never doubted that he was never far from her side.

"Hi, Ship."

"I want to offer you my condolences."

"No one died, Ship. You don't offer condolences because someone got dumped."

"I thought it was the appropriate word choice. Your intimate relationship with Taio has died. Never to be the same again. An ending to a love affair. The ending to—"

Eva threw up a hand. "Point taken. Thank you."

She wanted to ask if Taio knew where she was, then thought against it. He probably did, all he had to do was run a heat signature sweep of the palace and find her. He had no need to seek her out. Did not care. Did not miss her.

She shook her head, attempting to get those hurtful thoughts out of it. Her pity party ended two minutes ago.

She slapped her knees. "Better get this show on the road." She attempted to will her legs to straighten and support her weight.

"What show? Is the lack of food making you delusional? I found out humans cannot go more than two to three Earth days without food or water. I was monitoring you to make sure you did not die of starvation."

"How kind of you." She genuinely meant that. It was not often that someone looked out for her well-being. "I really appreciate it." Finally straightening, she reached out to a piece of equipment to stabilize herself.

"What do you plan to do now?"

What *was* she going to do? "I don't know, Ship."

\* \* \* \* \*

"Sir, Eva's heat signature showed up in the training hall," Jor'Dan said.

Taio inhaled sharply. She had been found. That was the best news he'd heard in a lifetime. He'd had everyone searching the palace from top to bottom. Everyone helped in the search except Ship, who had been tight-lipped since the announcement.

He was about to make the call to have the search extended outside, not believing or wanting to believe she was dead. That would have been the only reason as to why her heat signature would not have shown up.

171

He hadn't known it would hurt as it had to make the announcement. Looking at her made it worse. His first instinct had been to run over and hold her. It had taken all his resolve not to look at her again, for fear he would do just that.

Sonis needed this match. With Laconia behind the bonding, Sonis could finally be a thriving world. He had more important responsibilities to think of. It would be extremely selfish of him to make a decision with his cock instead of his head.

"How did she get into the training hall without being detected? We searched that entire area." He turned to Rasha.

"We didn't bother to look in the old equipment rooms," Rasha said. "The heat sensors were draining energy from the ionized weights held there. Remember, you had the sensors disabled. They've been unused for many cycles. If she was hiding in there we would not have picked up on her heat signature."

"She hid in there for two whole rotations?"

His initial relief was now turning to fury. He'd turned the entire palace upside down looking for her while she hid away. What did she hope to prove by this little stunt? Besides, Eva knew this day was coming. He still had to marry Princess Sa'Mya, who was none too happy that he put their ceremony on hold while he searched high and low for Eva.

Taio stormed the restroom as Eva was coming out. He didn't know if he should crush her close to his body or grab her, shaking some sense into her little human brain. When he reached her, he did neither.

"Do you know how much time I wasted looking for you?"

Eva blinked in surprise. She was red in the face, and she narrowed her eyes, peering at him through the slits. "I'm sorry to have *wasted* your time. But I don't recall needing to be found and I don't recall asking you to be the one to do it."

"I'm glad you are unharmed, Eva." Rasha stepped up, clearly trying to diffuse the situation.

Eva kept her eyes glaring at him. "I appreciate your concern, Rasha, but I was never in any danger."

"You could have been in danger. How were we to know you were safe while you were hiding in the equipment room? You are still my responsibility." Rasha clenched his fists at his sides.

"For your information, I was *not* hiding. I don't hide, not from you or from anyone else."

"If you weren't hiding, what were you doing?"

"I actually don't owe you an explanation. But if you must know, I was making plans."

"Plans?" he asked, perplexed. "Plans about what?"

"Plans about my future. If I have to be trapped here with you, I thought it would be a good idea to figure some things out."

"Trapped? You are not trapped!"

Rasha took a step to move in front of Taio. "Maybe we should allow you to have a nice warm bath, eat and then revisit this conversation later. Does that sound good?" Rasha took Eva's elbow and tried to lead her out the door.

Eva snatched her arm away and spun around. "I am too trapped. You told me you have complete authority over me and I can never leave! Where I come from, that's considered trapped!"

Taio straightened his shoulders. Never had anyone yelled or spoken to him as Eva was doing. Did she really feel forced to stay with him?

"You are free to go wherever you desire," Taio said calmly.

"Now, it would not be beneficial to say things we do not mean," Rasha interjected.

"I mean what I say, Rasha, do not involve yourself in matters that are not your concern." Rasha nodded once and stepped out of the way.

"Eva, you have plenty of credits in your account. Coyl and the others were not rich, but they had well-paying salaries. Once they attacked you, they immediately forfeited their worth to you. You have enough to be comfortable with for a while." He turned on his heel, but stopped before leaving. "I will have Mazel look for vacant properties on Sonis for you. If you don't find one to your liking, feel free to build one."

"I won't need her help," she said. Taio turned just in time to catch her squaring her shoulders. "If I'm free to go, then I'll go. Ship, will you help me find the first transport off Sonis?"

"Where is your destination?" Ship asked.

"Anywhere but here."

Taio walked away, not looking back. If she planned to run to Alexion, he would let her go.

# Chapter Twenty-Four

ഒ

"What day did you reschedule the ceremony for?" his mother asked. Her weariness was clearly visible on her face as she peered at him from the communication screen.

She'd called him to complain about his behavior. Apparently, no one wanted to be near him because his attitude was less than desirable these past three lunar cycles.

He hadn't even realized everyone was avoiding him. He'd been too wrapped up in his own thoughts to notice anything else. But the moment she brought up the ceremony, he instantly tuned her out. Apparently, they had now moved the discussion from his behavior to the ceremony.

"Taio! Pay attention to me. It is time for you to snap out of it and move on with your life. You have a beautiful mate-to-be who has been waiting patiently for you to come to your senses. You cannot continue to put her off," his mother said firmly.

Taio could hear the distress in his mother's voice. His mother, father and sister had returned home to the main planet awhile ago. When? He wasn't too certain about that, most of the guests had left when it became apparent there wouldn't be a bonding ceremony anytime soon. Kiehle left well before his parents—he still had a business to run.

"Taio!" his mother called out again. His eyes snapped back to the communication screen.

"Yes, Mother."

"Well? What is the new date?"

"I haven't set it yet."

"Tsk. That poor girl. What are you planning to do? Keep her hanging around while you mourn the loss of your lover?"

"I am not holding her hostage, she can leave whenever she wants."

She rolled her eyes. "Don't be an ass."

"Mother, you don't understand. I am still bonding with her. I can't afford not to, Sonis needs her. I am trying to get some things in order first. I felt rushed into it anyway."

"Pah. You were more than ready to mate with her. It's only after you let your little concubine go that you took this downward turn," she said. "I thought I had it figured out. I am partly to blame as well."

"You are not the blame for this. It was me. I wasn't honest with Eva from the beginning."

"No. I thought I knew what was best for you. I should have supported what I knew in my heart from the beginning."

"You knew about my feelings for her?"

"Ha! Everyone who has eyes knew how you felt about Eva and how she felt about you," she said. "And you are correct, I don't understand. I don't understand how you let her go so easily. If I had someone who loved me and I loved them back, I would have fought harder to hold onto it."

"But I'm king here. I have to do what's right for everyone. I have to think of more than just my needs."

"Oh I see, so who does it benefit if your staff is too afraid to approach you because you'll lash out at them? Who benefits if you have not completed one task? Who benefits when your business contacts are requesting not to deal with you? Who benefits if—"

"Mother! I get the idea."

"My sweet baby, I am just trying to get you to understand that if you are not happy, it does affect everyone. I just want you to be happy."

"Even if I want her, it could never be more than what it was. She's not royalty. She has nothing to offer Sonis. What would the other delegates think if I mated with a species that couldn't defend their own world?" He had been thinking about this ever since she left.

"I thought I raised you better than this," his mother said. "I wanted so much more for you, Kiehle and Saia. No matter how you were brought into this world, I wanted you all to make your own decisions and choices. To be able to weigh the good and the bad. When you left home and set up on Sonis, I was so proud of you."

"I know, Mother."

She raised her hand. "No, you don't. I wanted to do right by you. Who cares what those stuffy old dignitaries and council members think? You have the best defense system known to us. You have an entity that is as old as this galaxy at your side. And you had a female who loved you."

Taio hung his head. His mother was right. He had been so caught up in trying to do right by Sonis that he wasn't doing right by himself. So what if he mated with Eva? No one would dare think him weak, they would find out the hard way he wasn't.

He pushed back his chair and began to rise.

"Where are you going?"

"I am going to find Eva." His mother was right. He needed to get Eva back.

His mother smiled and blew a kiss at him. "Send me a new date for the ceremony!"

He found Sa'Mya lounging in the library with Yazmine lying at her side, playing with her long, golden tresses. He guessed Sa'Mya wouldn't be too heartbroken about what he was about to tell her. She seemed to prefer Yazmine's company to his anyway.

"Can we go somewhere and talk, alone?" He sent a dismissive glance toward her personal guard, Moira and Yazmine.

Sa'Mya had taken the news better than he could have imagined. "It was clear from the beginning the two of you were in love. We all knew it was a package deal and she was part of the package."

"I am sorry for making you wait all this time for a ceremony that will not take place."

Sa'Mya let out a heavy breath. "To be honest, it was a vacation for me. I enjoyed being here." She gave a sweeping glance around the old library that held millions of data files.

"You are welcome back anytime you want to visit."

Sa'Mya's eyes became distant. "Taio, I do have a favor to ask of you."

"Anything."

She shook her head. "I don't need the favor now, just promise you will grant it when I call you."

"Sa'Mya, I'm on the council, it can't be anything illegal," he said, warning her. He didn't like the idea of promising a favor without knowing what he was promising for.

"No." She shook her head again. "You have nothing to worry about on that end. I will need a favor and I want to be able to count on a friend." Something in her eyes compelled him to help her.

"You will be able to count on me."

Sa'Mya smiled. "Thank you." Then, as if it was an afterthought. "I will make sure that our previous arrangement is modified."

Taio had assumed that since there would not be a ceremony, their contract would be voided.

"I will still make sure that you have use of my transport vessels. Mind you, you won't be part-owner anymore and I want a percentage of the profits made when this little world of yours becomes a thriving attraction," Sa'Mya said.

"Thank you." He bowed his head. This was more than generous of her, especially since she wasn't obligated to him anymore.

"Anything for a friend." She bowed hers in return.

Taio had the feeling she was endearing herself to him for when she called in her "favor". He would worry about that later.

Leaving her, he returned to his personal quarters to pack his bag. He needed to go to Holis, praying that he wasn't too late.

"Ship! Get me Taraj Hazouto from Holis on the—"

He stopped mid-sentence. Ship was gone. He stopped what he was doing and ran to his office. He couldn't dial the code for Taraj Hazouto quick enough. He let out an extended breath as her face came into view.

"Greetings, Taraj." He bowed his head to the diplomat.

"Greetings, King Taio. What an honor it is for you to call upon me."

"The honor is all mine." He smiled. "I would appreciate it very much if you could let me speak with Eva."

"Eva?" she asked. "Why would Eva be here?"

"I assumed she was there with Alexion. Is she not?"

"I'm afraid not. We last spoke with her five rotations ago. She was going to Zolaris. She had news her friend, Allysan, was being held there," Taraj explained.

Taio blanched at the news. She was trekking around the galaxy with only Ship to take care of her.

"I don't understand, I thought she was with Alexion?"

"Why would she be with Alexion?"

"They shared a mutual attraction. I assumed when she left here she went running to him." Panic crept across his heart. Where was she? She was a human female, she didn't know anything about the dangers the universe held.

"You misunderstood, King Taio. Alexion does find her to be quite appealing, exotic even. But Eva did not share his feelings."

"But I saw them together a lot. There was more to their relationship than you are letting on."

"They had a friendship. Once Eva told us about her people, we felt compelled to help. Alexion came up with the idea of us setting up safe planets for the other humans. Alexion was planning it and I was using my contacts as a dignitary to find suitable sites. It was no more than a working relationship, I assure you. My brother cannot keep any secrets from me."

"I can't believe I let her leave on her own." He leaned back in his chair. "She could be in so much danger." He ran a hand through his tangled hair.

"Don't worry, Ship is taking good care of her. He would never leave her side. Not even for a minute. Especially since she is starting to show."

"Show what?"

"Her pregnancy, of course. Ship is extremely protective of her. She told me Ship has insisted this was going to be her last attempt to find Allysan before the baby is born."

Taio's mind froze. Pregnant? Baby?

Taraj's eyes widened in response. "King Taio, you did not know that she was pregnant?"

# Chapter Twenty-Five

ℬ

Eva sat slumped at the bar. This was the seventh dead end she had run into in the past six months. And not to mention her ankles were swelling. She looked at them in disgust and curled her lip. It was bad enough that she had been dumped, but dumped and fat? That was just plain wrong.

She was on an Interplanetary System Transport Vessel headed to nowhere. Well, it was going somewhere, but she was drifting. She couldn't find Ally, the few friends she made on Sonis were gone and, of course, no Taio. The only thing that kept her hopes somewhat up was the chance of finding Ally and reclaiming a little bit of the normalcy she lost. Now, with her belly growing bigger by the day and no Ally, she would need to go somewhere quiet to lick her wounds.

She wanted Ally, she wanted her friend back, but there was another reason that was more pressing. Ship gave her news that Ally had been sold and re-sold to as many as three different brothels throughout the galaxy. She needed to find her friend. Now.

This last lead on Ally had seemed as though it was finally going to be the one. But it turned out to be a bust. Ally had been sold yet again, this time to a private broker who would no doubt turn around and sell her again. Ship could track her, but it would take awhile for Ally to hit the grid again.

Eva thought highly of her fighting skills, but even she knew she wouldn't be able to launch a one-woman rescue mission this late in her pregnancy. Eva sighed as she thought about the delay. There was no way around it. She would need to resume the search after her son was born.

Ship had made her visit a medical healer on the first planet they visited after leaving Sonis. Although she didn't appreciate the entity making her do anything, she had relented. The medical healer told her she was carrying a son and so far he was healthy. The baby she carried was her first priority, finding Ally was her second.

On every planet she had been to, she inquired about ideal places to live and raise children. She had a few requirements in mind. The temperature had to be mild and sunny yearlong. The days had to match Earth's standard days as much as possible. She looked for a place where she and the baby would be safe living alone, and of course, it had to be in a different solar system than Sonis.

Somewhere far away.

Out of the corner of her eye, she spotted a male walking toward her. His blue-tinted lips sported a malicious grin. His translucent gray skin color, pointy ears and long, blond hair identified his species, Uurosolian. Since she was on her own, learning about different species was a requirement. The information she gathered on Uurosolians was that their race was known to be aggressive toward their females and very dangerous.

*Shit.* She kept her eyes on him while she let her hand slide to her blaster.

*Crap. Crap. Crap.* Transport rules, no weapons onboard. Her blaster was checked with her bag, she wouldn't be able to have it until they reached their final destination.

The transport lurched forward just slightly, enough to cause the Uurosolian's steps to falter and her side to bang against the countertop. She looked around to see if anything visible was going on. Nothing. She quickly dismissed the disruption. It was probably an air pocket or authorities scanning the vessel. They did this in hopes of catching fugitives or unapproved cargo.

Eva didn't linger on it, the transport would continue on its way once the scan was complete. She had bigger worries.

"Hello there." The Uurosolian slid into the chair next to hers, smiling viciously with a mouth full of pointy teeth.

"Hello yourself." She smiled back. "My name is Eva." She extended her hand to him. The last thing she needed was to hurt this guy's feelings and be entangled in some kind of physical altercation. Kill him with kindness. Kindness and lies.

His confident smile turned somewhat wary. Not the easy prey he suspected she was, Eva thought.

Hand still extended, she looked at his hand, then back at hers.

With a confused look on his face, the Uurosolian took her hand in his and Eva shook vigorously up and down.

"Eva," she said again. "And your name would be?"

"Losix." He nervously looked around the room as if she were setting him up.

She was sitting alone, looking depressed and beat down. She was sure he hoped to build her spirits up with sugarcoated words that would lead to an easy lay. She didn't appear to be the same person he spotted a few moments ago.

She kept a smile on her face and shook his hand vigorously. "Losix. That's a real strong name. I like strong names. You're from Uurose, right? I've heard of your people."

She stopped shaking his hand but held it tight in her grip. She stroked it with her free hand and leaned closer to him. "Even saw a few since I've been traveling the galaxy."

"Umm... I mistook you for an old acquaintance. I'm sorry to impose on you," he replied quickly.

He was trying to free his hand from her grasp when a bloodcurdling war cry erupted behind her.

Eva jumped from her seat and instinctively got behind Losix, shielding herself from whatever was about to happen.

"I. Will. Rip. You. To. Shreds. Uurosolian." Each word dripped with hate. "Do you *dare* touch my mate?"

Eva slowly recognized the voice behind the madness. Taio?

"I apologize. I was just telling the female that I mistook her for an old acquaintance. I meant no harm." As he spoke, Losix reached behind his back, trying to grab a hold of her. Eva held the back of his shirt tight in her fist.

"Why does she hide behind you?"

"I am trying to free myself from her. I have been trying to free myself ever since we greeted."

Eva unclenched her fist, and with nervous energy, began to smooth out the wrinkles of his shirt.

"You let her stroke you!" Taio's voice bellowed across the room. Eva could feel his boots stomping closer to her direction.

*Oh crap.*

Losix jumped up and stepped out of the way, exposing her to Taio's fury. She gave the Uurosolian an annoyed look. He shrugged and made his way to the exit.

Her knees weakened at the sight of him. He seemed taller than she remembered, bigger and a whole lot meaner. He was in need of a shave, and when he stopped in front of her, she smelled the stench coming from his body and clothes and decided he needed a bath too.

"I am not your mate. You made that quite clear," she said calmly, surprising even herself.

"You are my mate. You carry my child." His voice was loud, staking his claim.

So he had found out about the baby.

"For your information, that does not make us mates! Where I'm from, we call that a baby mama!" She fumbled for her chair. Her knees were definitely getting weak now. "I'm not your slave anymore."

She slid into her chair. "You gave me my freedom. I have witnesses."

Taio stepped closer to her, cradling her face in his hands.

"You are not my slave. You never were, but you are mine. You always will be. This is mine." He rubbed his hand across her distended belly.

She hung her head low, tears ran down her cheeks. "No, Taio. I'm not yours. I can't watch you and Princess Sa'Mya together and stay with you. Not even for the baby. You can't make me do it."

Taio gathered her off the stool, cradling her in his thick arms. "I would never ask you to do something so foolish. You will be my mate."

Eva looked at him through tear-soaked eyes.

"How can I be your mate?"

"I love you and you carry my child."

"You love me?"

"Yes, and if you do not come back with me, Kiehle will drag this entire transport back to Sonis and keep it there until you change your mind."

"You put a hold on the transport?" She finally looked around. Everyone watched her and Taio with stunned looks on their faces. But aside from that, the transport guards were all being held in headlocks by Taio's crew.

"I need you back. I came prepared for a fight. I had to first convince Ship to let me board to speak with you. Eva, I want you by my side. Just you, my little one. My queen."

"Taio, I don't know if I can trust you again. What you did…it hurt."

"Eva, please. I would do anything to have you back with me, where you belong."

"We'll be mated?"

"Yes. We will sign the bonding contract as soon as we return to Sonis."

Eva put up her hand. "I want to be able to continue to train with the guards."

"Eva, that is not a queen's place." She turned her back. "But one item that we can add to the contract."

She wasn't giving in that easy. She turned back around. "I want a say in our son's upbringing."

"Son?" He fumbled for the chair. Her insides instantly melted. He would love their child with all his heart.

"Yes, I'm carrying your son and I want equal say in his upbringing."

"This is unheard of." He shook his head. "This is a father's responsibility."

Eva's lips twitched. She knew she would lose that battle. She hoped for it. "Okay. If I can't have equal say in the raising of our son, then I want an enlightenment ceremony."

"That is out of the question."

She held up her finger. "We are negotiating. If I can't have equal say in the upbringing of our son, I should at least have an enlightenment ceremony."

He sat back and crossed his arms. "I'll think about it."

Eva sat back as well. "When you come to a conclusion, let me know. I'll have Ship inform you which planet the baby and I settle down on."

"All right. You can have an enlightenment ceremony. *After* our son is born."

Eva hauled back and punched him as hard as she could in his muscle-ripped stomach.

"What was that for?"

"That's for upsetting me and putting me through hell."

"I'm sorry, little one."

"Queen," she corrected.

Eva buried her face in his stomach and held on tight. She would never let him go. Their son would grow up in a loving

186

two-parent household. But most importantly, he would grow up in a family.

Her family.

# Epilogue

**ဢ**

Eva sat cross-legged on a blanket that covered the sandy ground next to the training field. Her eyes fluttered closed as she tilted her head up toward the bright suns, welcoming the rays on the tattoo that circled around her right eye. Taio had explained that the heat generated from the suns' rays would help to dry and heal the elaborate tattoos that she now possessed. Having undergone the enlightenment ceremony a couple of weeks beforehand, the two intricate designs of *varitizars* were healing nicely, although the skin underneath the tattoos itched something fierce. Later, when she found some time to herself, she planned to lie naked in the private royal gardens to expose the bottom part of the designs that covered her torso, chest and neck to the suns' rays.

A cry from the training field jolted her back to the present.

"That's the one I have my eye on," Lo'Ren said. She was sitting next to Eva watching the guards train. "He just doesn't know it yet."

Eva followed Lo'Ren's line of vision to one of Taio's new royal guards. "What about Ankon?"

Lo'Ren snorted. "Who says I can't have my eyes on both of them?"

Eva laughed, making the child sleeping soundly next to her shift on the blanket. She hadn't dared sit close enough to the field that she or her son, Josanis, could be injured. Even though the guards on the field would as soon cut off their arms than to cause harm to Josanis, she didn't want to hear Taio's mouth regarding all of the possible dangers that the training field held and all the many ways Josanis could be injured.

At the thought of her and Taio's two-year-old son, Eva reached over and rested a hand on his back, feeling his soft, rhythmic breathing. Eva didn't worry at all about the suns' rays damaging his skin as it had done hers years ago, the sun-protective clothing he wore would prevent that from happening. She smoothed a lock of raven-black hair away from his forehead and curled it around his ear. Lying at his side was a much smaller version of a *jango* that Taio had specially made for his first-born son. The stubborn child carried it everywhere he went, insisting that it stay at his side, even in sleep.

Josanis had been the first interspecies union, but he would not be the last. It was amazing to find out that humans could be the welcomed solution to the Drazlan and Sonis breeding problem. Taio had brought more human women of childbearing age to live and settle on both Sonis and Drazlan.

Taio and his father had bought human females from slave traders and even paid the women handsomely to settle on Sonis and Drazlan. The women had all been happy enough to be granted freedom. But they gained much more, a place to call home, shelter and the possibility to find their own protectors and raise families. Eva was more than happy to be tasked with the job of making sure that all their needs had been met, that the women assimilated into their new culture with ease and that the people of Drazlan and Sonis also understood their new inhabitants.

Her thoughts were interrupted when a purplish-haze obstructed her view of the training field. The first time she had seen the unfamiliar haze, she had thought her eyes had failed her. Why else could she see a disturbance that had the same look of purple-heat waves moving throughout the palace and not anyone else? When she had asked Taio and Lo'Ren about the visual disturbance, they had all denied that they could see anything. As it turned out, her human eyes could detect the entity while other species could not.

"Hello, Ship," she said. "This must be real important if you are out and about."

"Hi, Ship," Lo'Ren said, taking her cue from Eva.

Although Ship thrived and preferred to travel through electrical currents, it wasn't necessary to do so. As long as he didn't stay away from electrical currents for great lengths of time, he would survive. Now that she knew what to look for, Eva always caught him traveling inconspicuously throughout the palace.

"Yes, it is very important. But if you do not appreciate that I am exposing myself to the elements, then I will go back inside the palace walls."

"Don't be so temperamental. I was being sarcastic. I do appreciate that you've come outside and risked fresh air to talk with me."

Eva held back her smile in hopes Ship didn't catch that she was being sarcastic yet again.

"Thank you for your concern," Ship replied. She smiled then. He hadn't caught on to it. "When are you going to tell Taio about your pregnancy?"

Eva and Lo'Ren gasped in unison. Eva's hand went to rest on her stomach. "How did you know? I haven't even told the healers yet."

Lo'Ren scrunched her face. "Or me."

"The same way I knew the first time. I can see the other energy…life force within your abdomen. Although small, it is there," Ship replied.

Eva sighed. "I'm sorry." She grabbed Lo'Ren's hand and gave it a small squeeze. "I wanted to wait until after the enlightenment ceremony to tell Taio. And then I kept thinking that I could receive news about Ally any day."

"That is no reason to deceive your mate, Eva."

"I know. But Ship, what if we do get word about her? Taio would never let me go while I'm pregnant."

"You are correct. But you still mustn't deceive him."

Eva huffed. "Okay, I'll tell him. I guess I've been putting it off longer than I should have."

"You won't have to go far, he is on his way to you," Ship said.

Eva looked up to see Taio walking toward her in the distance and Ship floating back to the palace before finally disappearing. Taio moved with such predatory grace. *That's my man.* Eva moaned under her breath.

Lo'Ren rolled her eyes. "It's a wonder that you don't *stay* pregnant." Lo'Ren gathered Josanis in her arms. He whimpered in his sleep and she placed a light kiss on his forehead. "I'll take Josanis inside so that you both can have privacy."

"Thanks, Lo."

"Don't mention it. And I really mean it this time, don't mention it. *Disgusting.*" She stuck out her tongue.

Eva laughed as Lo'Ren and Josanis left. Lo'Ren stopped to let Taio kiss his son before she continued to the palace.

"Taking a break?" Eva asked as he reached her.

Taio settled next to her on the ground. "I thought I would spend time with my family for a while. But I see Lo'Ren has stolen one member away."

Eva beamed from ear to ear and leaned on him. *Family.*

"You know, we never had a conversation about how large we want our family to be."

He tilted his head to the side. "I never imagined I would have ever had a choice in the matter."

He began to run his hand through her hair, playing and twisting it through his fingers.

"So…"

"So what?" he asked.

"How many children do you want?"

"Eva, I thought having one child was unattainable. I would be happy with whatever number the Ancients bless us with."

The fingers that he had twirling through her hair suddenly stopped. "Eva? Are you..."

She looked up to him sheepishly. "Yes."

He crushed her body to his. He buried his face in her hair and sniffled. "Royal guards do not cry."

She smiled as her eyes misted over. "But I can."

Taio rolled over on her, pressing her back onto the blanket. "If you weren't my queen, I'd take you right here," he whispered into her ear.

She wrapped her arms and legs around him. "I'll be your concubine any day."

*Also by A.M. Griffin*

ഔ

*eBooks:*

Dangerously Mine

Dangerously Yours

Fondled and Gobbled: Back for More  *(anthology)*

Fondled and Gobbled: Going Back for Seconds *(anthology)*

## About A.M. Griffin

∞

A.M. Griffin is a wife who rarely cooks, mother of three, dog owner (and sometimes dog owned), a daughter, sister, aunt and friend. She's a hard worker whose two favorite outlets are reading and writing. She enjoys reading everything from mystery novels to historical romances and of course fantasy romance. She is a believer in the unbelievable, open to all possibilities from mermaids in our oceans and seas, angels in the skies and intelligent life forms in distant galaxies. She has multi-publications in other genres under a different pen name.

∞

The author welcomes comments from readers. You can find her website and email address on her author bio page at www.ellorascave.com.

## Tell Us What You Think

We appreciate hearing reader opinions about our books. You can email us at Service@ellorascave.com (when contacting Customer Service, be sure to state the book title and author).

# Why an electronic book?

We live in the Information Age—an exciting time in the history of human civilization, in which technology rules supreme and continues to progress in leaps and bounds every minute of every day. For a multitude of reasons, more and more avid literary fans are opting to purchase e-books instead of paper books. The question from those not yet initiated into the world of electronic reading is simply: *Why?*

1. *Price.* An electronic title at Ellora's Cave Publishing runs anywhere from 40% to 75% less than the cover price of the exact same title in paperback format. Why? Basic mathematics and cost. It is less expensive to publish an e-book (no paper and printing, no warehousing and shipping) than it is to publish a paperback, so the savings are passed along to the consumer.

2. *Space.* Running out of room in your house for your books? That is one worry you will never have with electronic books. For a low one-time cost, you can purchase a handheld device specifically designed for e-reading. Many e-readers have large, convenient screens for viewing. Better yet, hundreds of titles can be stored within your new library—on a single microchip. There are a variety of e-readers from different manufacturers. You can also read e-books on your PC or laptop computer. (Please note that Ellora's Cave does not endorse any specific brands.

You can check our website at www.ellorascave.com for information we make available to new consumers.)

3. *Mobility.* Because your new e-library consists of only a microchip within a small, easily transportable e-reader, your entire cache of books can be taken with you wherever you go.

4. *Personal Viewing Preferences.* Are the words you are currently reading too small? Too large? Too... ANNOYING? Paperback books cannot be modified according to personal preferences, but e-books can.

5. *Instant Gratification.* Is it the middle of the night and all the bookstores near you are closed? Are you tired of waiting days, sometimes weeks, for bookstores to ship the novels you bought? Ellora's Cave Publishing sells instantaneous downloads twenty-four hours a day, seven days a week, every day of the year. Our webstore is never closed. Our e-book delivery system is 100% automated, meaning your order is filled as soon as you pay for it.

Those are a few of the top reasons why electronic books are replacing paperbacks for many avid readers.

As always, Ellora's Cave welcomes your questions and comments. We invite you to email us at Service@ellorascave.com or write to us directly at Ellora's Cave Publishing Inc., 1056 Home Avenue, Akron, OH 44310-3502.

MAKE EACH-DAY MORE *EXCITING* WITH OUR

# ELLORA'S CAVEMEN
## CALENDAR

☥ WWW.ELLORASCAVE.COM ☥

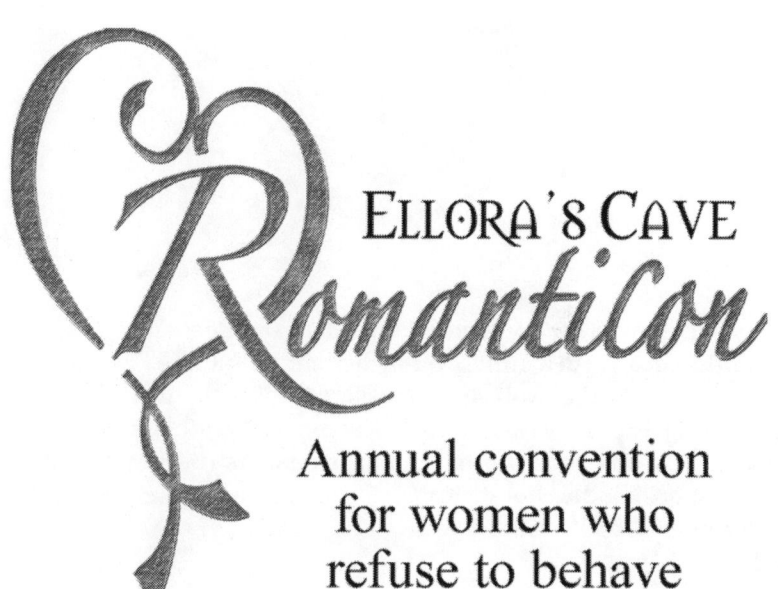

ELLORA'S CAVE

*Romanticon*

Annual convention
for women who
refuse to behave

www.ECRomanticon.com
For additional info contact: conventions@ellorascave.com

Discover for yourself why readers can't get enough of the multiple award-winning publisher Ellora's Cave. Be sure to visit EC on the web at www.ellorascave.com to find erotic reading experiences that will leave you breathless. You can also find our books at all the major e-tailers (Barnes & Noble, Amazon Kindle, Sony, Kobo, Google, Apple iBookstore, All Romance eBooks, and others).

# www.ellorascave.com

Made in the USA
Lexington, KY
27 February 2014